Cindy looked away for _____ —
a moment she'll re _____
of her life . . .

"I'm fly-y-ying!" Hei_____ _ed again, as we swooped back up the arc of the Ferris wheel.

My eyes were still on Veronica and Trevor when Heidi somehow let go of her cotton candy. Without thinking, she jumped up to catch it, and that's when it happened.

The safety bar gave way.

Heidi screamed my name. I'll remember that scream, that moment, for as long as I live.

I reached out for her, just touching the edge of her red and white sweatshirt, but it all happened so fast, and her little body was beyond my grasp, as Heidi flew through the air and hurtled toward the earth.

Get Well Soon, Little Sister

*This book is for my favorite singing group,
the Bloody Nieces—Maia Gottesfeld,
Shannon Berman, and Juliet Berman.*

You guys rule!

Text copyright © 1996 by Cherie Bennett.

Published by Troll Communications L.L.C.

Printed in the United States of America.

10 9 8 7 6 5 4 3 2

HOPE HOSPITAL

Get Well Soon, Little Sister

BY CHERIE BENNETT

Troll

CHAPTER 1

"What should I wear for the first day of eighth grade tomorrow?" I asked the huge Mickey Mouse clock on the wall of the bedroom I share with my little sister, Heidi. "Tell me the truth. Be brutal."

Normally I would have been asking my best friend, Jennifer Munson, but Jennifer had the nerve to move clear across the country with her family during the summer. Jennifer and I had been best friends since we were both three and she barfed on me at preschool. Ten years. Ten years of sharing everything, and then just because her dad got transferred she left

Hope forever, and moved to San Francisco. Sure. Leave me behind in the tiny town of Hope, Michigan, and move to a city that I have heard is only the coolest place on the entire planet.

The traitor.

Which was why I was forced to ask this important question of good ole Mickey, who just kept smiling and ticking away on my wall.

"Should I try to stand out or should I try to fit in?" I said, as if talking to a clock was a perfectly normal thing to do. "I mean, you know what it's like not to fit in, yourself. After all, you're short. And you're black. And you're a mouse."

"Uh, Cindy, if that clock answers you I'm going to be really scared," my brother Clark smirked from the doorway.

Just because Clark is sixteen and to-die-for cute (according to Jennifer, anyway, but don't get me started on Jennifer again), he thinks he's the coolest thing on two legs. Ha.

"How about you pretend you're really Superman and fly away?" I suggested. My brother Clark is named after Clark Kent—you know, Superman's name when he wasn't being Superman. That may seem bizarre to you, but my name is really

Cinderella, Cindy for short. I guess I don't have to tell you who I'm named after.

"I'll help you pick something out to wear," Clark offered.

I narrowed my eyes and put my hands on my hips. Clark is not normally so nice to me. "What's the catch?" I asked him.

"No catch," he insisted. He walked over to my closet. "Okay, you're a shrimp—"

"Petite," I corrected him.

"Yeah, whatever," he said breezily, pawing through my clothes. "Let's see, what looks decent on a thirteen-year-old girl with blond curly hair and blue eyes who looks like she's about ten—"

"I do not!" I cried, stepping on the toe of his sneakers.

"Well, basically the situation is pretty hopeless," Clark said cheerfully. He pulled a denim jumper out of my closet and held it up. "This?"

"I hate that," I said with a sigh. "I wore that when I really *was* ten."

"And it still fits," Clark pointed out wickedly. "Hey, maybe you're going to stay four foot eleven forever!"

"I'm five feet tall," I insisted, grabbing the jumper and stuffing it back in my closet. "Mickey Mouse was more help than you are." I threw myself down on my bed and grabbed my Raggedy Ann doll. "I wish I could get something new. Just one thing . . ."

"We can't afford it," Clark said.

"Duh," I replied. "Like I don't know."

"Don't say anything to Dad about it," Clark warned. "He'll feel bad."

"Cindy, my throat hurts," my little sister said, padding into the room. She was named after this famous novel about a girl who goes to live with her grandfather in the Alps—these mountains in Switzerland. Guess what her name is.

"You always say that," I told her, as she climbed onto my bed and snuggled against me.

"Because it always hurts," Heidi explained, running her fingers through Raggedy Ann's hair. "I don't think I should go to kindergarten tomorrow."

"But it's your very first day of school," Clark pointed out, sitting across from us on Heidi's bed. "Don't you want to go to school like a big girl?"

"No," Heidi replied.

The phone rang out in the hall. "It's for me," Clark yelled, and dashed out of the room.

"I bet it's Melanie," Heidi said, wrinkling her

nose. Melanie is Clark's latest girlfriend. She is a cheerleader and has the brain of a flea. She calls Clark about seventy times a day.

"Want me to pick out something for you to wear to school tomorrow?" I offered, smoothing Heidi's hair out of her face.

She shook her head no. "I don't think I should go, honest."

"You don't need to be scared," I told her gently. "It'll be fun."

"But my throat hurts," Heidi insisted.

I sighed. This throat thing of Heidi's had been going on for about a month. Dad had taken her to see the pediatrician twice, and both times he said her throat was perfectly fine. But see, I knew the real reason she kept saying her throat hurt.

It was because of Mom dying.

Our mom died four years ago. She had throat cancer, and it started out as a sore throat. Of course, Heidi was only a baby, and she doesn't even remember Mom, but she'd heard people tell the story so many times—how Mom just had this bad sore throat and it wouldn't go away and by the time she found out it was cancer it was too late to save her—so Heidi keeps thinking that now she has a sore throat and she's going to die.

Just like Mom.

"Open up and say 'ah'," I told Heidi. She did. I peered into her open mouth. "Looks perfectly healthy."

"Then why does it hurt?" Heidi asked in a little voice.

"I'll tell you what," I said. "We'll lay out your clothes for school tomorrow, and then we'll go downstairs and have ice cream. I bet that will help your throat."

After we laid out Heidi's pink T-shirt, pink and blue plaid skirt, and pink tights, we went downstairs to forage for junk food. Clark was standing in front of the refrigerator, eating the last of the ice cream directly from the carton.

"Hey!" I screamed. "No fair!"

"I got here first," he pointed out, scraping the last spoonful out of the bottom.

"Hey, kids! This is awesome!" Dad yelled, running into the kitchen. "I just juggled four apples at once for the very first time!"

"Clark ate all the ice cream!" Heidi squealed.

Dad was too intent on his apple-juggling to pay any attention. "We're talking circus-quality juggling, here!" Dad flipped the four apples into the air.

"But, Daddy—" Heidi began.

"I started with scarves, you know? Apples are a lot harder!"

"Daddy, my throat hurts and I want ice cream!" Heidi whimpered.

"Maybe I can do a spin-move," Dad went on. "Okay, I'm going to try it. Here goes—" He spun around in a circle and managed to catch the apples at the same time. "Whoa, I did it! Hey, did you ever see those guys who can take a bite out of the apple while they—"

"I probably have cancer right this minute!" Heidi shrieked at the top of her lungs.

That finally got Dad's attention. My dad is a great guy and he really loves us, but he's kind of . . .well, the truth is he acts like a big kid. He's a pediatric social worker at Hope Hospital. That means he works with the little kids there, and helps them with their problems. The sick kids love him—he dresses up as a clown for them, and puts on all kinds of shows. The truth is that usually I feel like I'm more grown-up than Dad. Which is why I have to kind of be a mother to Heidi most of the time. This is just the way it is.

Dad caught the apples and set them on the kitchen table. Then he knelt down and put his arms around Heidi. "You don't have cancer, honey," he said gently.

"How do you know?" Heidi asked, her eyes huge.

"Because the doctor checked you out twice, remember?" Dad reminded her.

"It could have happened since then," Heidi pointed out.

"I'm going over to Melanie's," Clark said quickly, and he snuck out the back door. That really made me mad, how he ran away whenever anything serious was going on. And Dad never stopped him.

"Honey, little girls don't get cancer," Dad told Heidi.

I hated when Dad lied to Heidi like that. Little kids *do* get cancer sometimes. Dad worked with them at the hospital.

"How about if we order a pizza?" Dad suggested brightly.

"We had pizza for dinner," Heidi reminded him.

"Just testing you!" Dad said, tickling Heidi in the ribs. "We'll pile in the car and go out for ice cream, okay, sweetie?"

"Clark just took the car," I pointed out.

"He did? When?" Dad asked, looking around.

"When he said he was going to Melanie's

about two minutes ago and you didn't say a word," I said, folding my arms.

"Okay, so we'll call him at Melanie's house and ask him to bring home some ice cream. No need to get bent out of shape!" Dad said cheerfully. Dad is always cheerful. Sometimes I wonder if it's real, you know? Jennifer used to say that he was still covering up his sadness over Mom's death. Jennifer is very deep.

I really, really, really miss Jennifer.

Sometimes even more than I miss Mom.

Dad called Melanie's house, then he read Heidi a story. I went back upstairs and finally figured out what to wear to my first day back to school—a flannel baby-doll dress, tights, and hiking boots. After a while I heard Clark come home with the ice cream, but I didn't go back downstairs. I just lay on my bed, staring up at the ceiling, wondering about a million things. What would it be like to finally be in the highest grade at Hope Middle School? Would I make the gymnastics team—maybe even (please, God) be captain? Would I ever, ever have a boyfriend, preferably Trevor Wayne, the cutest guy in our class, who treated me like a bud instead of like a girl?

And finally, how was I ever going to go on without Jennifer?

CHAPTER 2

As soon as I got off the school bus the next morning, the first person I saw was Trevor Wayne. He got out of a red Mustang driven by his older brother, Chris, who zoomed off toward Hope High down the road.

Trevor and I had known each other ever since his family moved to Hope, which was five years earlier. Most everyone who lives in Hope has something to do with Hope Hospital, which is a large, pretty famous hospital for such a small town. Trevor's dad is a doctor, a pulmonary specialist. That has something to do with the lungs.

Trevor had been gorgeous even way back then, when he was only seven years old. He's also really nice, and smart, and he's the best tennis player I know. We would pal around sometimes—usually when he was between girlfriends.

Sigh.

"Wow, great car," I told Trevor, trying to sound a lot more casual than I felt. Trevor had grown about four inches over the summer. Now he was about five feet seven inches, with dark brown hair that fell into his eyes, the cutest dimple in his chin, the hugest brown eyes, a great tan, and—

"Yo, Winters, I missed you!" Trevor said, shifting his backpack around so that it hung loosely off one arm. "Have a good summer?"

"Yeah, sure," I told him, pretending I didn't mind at all that he called me by my last name like I was a guy or something. I hadn't seen Trevor all summer because his family had gone to Hawaii, where his dad had rented an isolated house so he could write some important medical textbook.

"Weird to see you without Jennifer," Trevor said, shaking the hair out of his eyes.

"Yeah." I sighed.

"How's she doing?"

I shrugged morosely. "According to her letters she loves San Francisco and she's having a great time."

"Can you blame her?" Trevor asked with a grin.

"Yes," I replied. "The least she could do is be miserable without me."

We walked up the steps to the school together. I looked around out of the corner of my eye, hoping kids would see Trevor Wayne walking me, Cindy Winters, into school. People knew we were buds, but maybe they would think it was more than that, and my status would go up big-time.

Not that I'm not popular, because I do okay. I mean, I'm not mega-popular, like Krystal Franklin or the other head cheerleader, Dawn McKnight, but I get along with everyone. I probably could have been a cheerleader, since I'm really, really good at gymnastics, but I didn't try out. Sometimes I wish I had, and other times I think the cheerleaders are really stupid and shallow.

"Who'd you get for English?" Trevor asked me as we walked into the school.

"Compton," I told him, rolling my eyes. Everyone knew that Mr. Compton was the toughest teacher in our school. He taught one of the two advanced-placement English classes—basically English for smart kids. I'm smart—or at least that's what all my teachers keep saying.

"Hey, me too," Trevor said with a grin. "Cool."

Cool? Trevor thought it was cool that we were in the same English class? Could it possibly be because he liked me? I mean, *liked* me–liked me, as in realized I was an actual *girl?*

"So, where's your locker this year?" I asked him, since we'd gotten new locker assignments in the mail the week before.

"B–17," he told me as we rounded the corner.

"I got B–18!" I exclaimed, which meant by chance my new locker was right next to his. Were things going my way or what?

"Hey, Wayne, man, how you doing?" Al Churchill yelled from across the hall. "Can you believe we're back here?"

"Same old, same old!" Trevor called back cheerfully.

"Hi, Trevor!" Krystal Franklin called, giving him a simpering grin.

"Hey, Krystal," he called back.

Krystal looked very cute in a short skirt

and a lightweight sweater that showed her curves had gotten even curvier over the summer. I looked down at my flat chest and sighed.

Trevor nudged me with his shoulder. "You're lookin' good, Winters," he told me.

"Yeah, right," I snorted. I stopped in front of my locker and pulled out the paper that had my new locker combination on it.

"No, seriously," Trevor said. "You look cute."

"I do?" I asked faintly.

"Yeah," he said, twirling the lock on his locker.

"Excuse me, is this locker B–19? There's no number on the locker."

A tall, slender, really pretty girl with long, perfectly straight brown hair stood there looking at me. She had on faded jeans that fit her to perfection, a white T-shirt, and a blazer that looked as if it cost more than my entire wardrobe. Diamond studs danced in her ears.

"Yeah," I replied, giving her a friendly smile. "I'm B–18, so that has to be B–19."

"Someone wrote over the numbers," she explained.

I looked down the row of lockers. She was right. Some moron had scribbled over the numbers with Magic Marker, misnumbering them.

"Some subhuman thought that was hilarious, I suppose," I told her. "I'm Cindy Winters. You're new, right?"

The girl nodded coolly. "I'm Veronica Langley," she said, in a soft, serious voice. She pushed some of her perfect hair behind one ear. "We just moved to Hope."

"Yeah, you'll love Hope," I said brightly. "There's, like so much to do here. You can watch the traffic lights change. Watch paint dry. Root for our football team, the Cougars—

"I hate football," Veronica said, reading her locker combination off her computer printout.

"Oh, well, lucky for you the games aren't mandatory," I pointed out, hoping she would smile or something.

She didn't.

"So, where'd you move here from?" I asked her, leaning against my locker.

"New York," she explained. "My mother is a pediatrician. That's a—"

"I know what it is," I said quickly. "A doctor who treats kids."

"Right," Veronica agreed. "Anyway, she's the new head of pediatrics at Hope Hospital."

"My dad works there," I told her. "He's a pediatric social worker. Hey, they'll probably be working together!"

"Possibly," Veronica said. "Although doctors don't usually interact with social workers very much."

Well, excuse me, I wanted to say. Although I felt like just walking away from her, something made me give friendship one more try. I don't know why—I'm just friendly, I guess. And I figured being new in a town like Hope, where most of us had known each other forever, wasn't the easiest thing in the world. It wouldn't be like being a new kid in, say, San Francisco, where a person could make a new best friend instantly just because so many people were new.

"So, are you in eighth?" I asked nicely. Nicely, mind you. If she was going to dis me one more time it wouldn't be because I hadn't given her every opportunity to be friendly.

"Yes," Veronica said, stashing her books in her locker.

"So are we," Trevor put in. "Hi," he added, grinning at her.

Trevor. I had forgotten about Trevor.

"Oh, this is Trevor Wayne," I said lamely.

He was making eye contact with Veronica big-time.

"Hello," Veronica said, like she could care less that Trevor looks like a movie star.

"So, what's your first class?" Trevor asked, smoothly maneuvering around me so that he stood next to Veronica.

She peered at her computer printout. "Social studies," she reported. "With . . ." she squinted her eyes and tried to read the messy computer print. "Ferris? Ferrit? I can't read it."

"Ferrill," Trevor said. "I'm in that class, too. I'll show you where it is."

"All right," Veronica agreed. She sounded as if she was doing Trevor a favor, sort of like royalty talking to a peasant. And he didn't even seem to mind.

"Hey, I'm in that class, too!" I exclaimed.

But Trevor and Veronica didn't hear me. They had already walked off down the hall. Together.

"And so, for the first project of the semester I will be assigning partners to work together," Ms. Ferrill said, clasping her hands together with excitement.

I sighed. Ms. Ferrill was the kind of teacher who got really excited about her work. Or should I say *our* work. She had already assigned us to read ten pages of our social studies textbook and we had a paper due in two weeks.

"As you know," Ms. Ferrill continued, "we're exploring racism and how it affects our society. You and your partner will be able to use any creative form you like— write an essay, build a model, write a play—on this topic."

This was what I got for being in honors classes. The honors teachers always wanted us to be creative. Sometimes it was really a pain. I looked over at Trevor, but he was looking at the new girl, Veronica. She was totally ignoring Trevor, writing notes in a new notebook with a felt-tip pen.

Annie Singleton raised her hand and waved it around until Ms. Ferrill called on her.

"Yes?"

"Can we pick our own partner?" Annie asked hopefully. Obviously she wanted to pair up with Pete Freed, her boyfriend.

"Not this time, Annie," Ms. Ferrill replied.

"Give her Charbutt!" Danny Crusier called from the back of the room. "She wants Charbutt bad!"

"Shut up," I hissed at Danny. I really can't

stand it when kids are cruel. Erwin Charbutt is the school nerd. He looks as awful as his name. He's really brilliant, but no one seems to care about that unless they want to copy one of his papers or something. His dad is a famous doctor at Hope Hospital.

"Let me read off the list of partners," Ms. Ferrill continued. "As soon as I'm done you'll have ten minutes of class time left to meet with your partner so that you can begin to plan your project. Remember, this project is worth twenty-five percent of your first quarter grade!"

Ms. Ferrill began to read from her list, and I snuck another look over at Trevor. I sent up a quick prayer to get him as a partner. It would be so great. We'd have to spend a lot of time together. He'd tell me I was cute again, and then he'd take me in his arms and—

"—Cindy Winters and Veronica Langley," Ms. Ferrill called out.

No. Please. Not her.

I hated her. I had tried to be nice to her and she had iced me out big-time. Clearly she was a total snob and I didn't want to have anything to do with her.

"All right," Ms. Ferrill called out. "Get together with your partner, everyone. I'm expecting some really creative things out of you guys!"

I looked over at Veronica, who was putting her felt-tip pen into her backpack, not even glancing in my direction. Well, I wasn't going to be the first one to move. No way. Let her get her butt out of her seat and come over to me.

I waited.

Nothing happened.

"Cindy, Veronica is waiting," Ms. Ferrill said, nodding in Veronica's direction.

"Oh, great," I said under my breath. "Just terrif." I got up and marched over to Veronica.

Trevor got there first.

"Too bad we're not partners," Trevor told her, leaning casually against the desk next to her.

She shrugged her royal shoulders at him, keeping her eyes down toward her backpack.

"Excuse me," I said in a loud voice. "I have to plan this stupid thing with Veronica."

"See ya," Trevor told her, like I didn't even exist. Then he sauntered off to meet with his partner.

"Look, I'm not so thrilled about working

with you either, okay?" I said nastily. "Let's just forget that you seem to hate my guts and get to work on this thing."

No reply.

I don't get mad very easily, but when I do I have a ferocious temper. And right at that moment I was ready to reach over and wring Veronica Langley's perfect neck.

"Hello!" I called. "Is anyone home?"

No answer.

"You are such a snob!" I exploded. I would have said more—I was really ready to just let her have it—until I saw why she was keeping her eyes down toward her desk, why she wasn't saying a word.

Veronica Langley was crying.

CHAPTER 3

What made me do it, I'll never know. But I ran up to Ms. Ferrill's desk, grabbed two hall passes, grabbed Veronica, and pushed her out the door toward the girls' john. Fortunately, for once, no one was in there.

"Now you can cry in peace," I told her, grabbing some toilet paper off the roll in the first stall.

"I'm okay," Veronica said. "Really."

"Then why is your lower lip trembling like that?" I pointed out.

She gulped hard. "I'm not usually very emotional."

I shrugged.

"It's just that . . .well, my parents just got divorced. And I had to leave all my friends behind in New York to move here with my mom . . ."

"That stinks," I agreed, leaning against the wall.

"My dad is back in New York," she continued, nervously twisting the toilet paper into little paper points. "He's a doctor, too. My parents used to work at the same hospital. Now they never want to see each other again."

She looked over at me. "I won't even get to see my dad until Thanksgiving. Or any of my friends. What am I supposed to do in Hope, Michigan? How could my mother do this to me?"

"Well, she didn't do it to *you*, exactly—"

"Next year I would have gone to the High School of Performing Arts," Veronica continued. "I'm a ballet dancer. I could probably get into City Ballet eventually, if I was still in New York. Now what am I supposed to do?"

"There's a *dance* school on Rutgers Road—"

"A dance school?" Veronica repeated in a withering voice, as if I was the dumbest thing walking.

"Okay, so you're way beyond Miss Faye's School of Dance in Hope, Michigan, I get the picture," I replied testily. I glanced at my watch. "We have to get back to class, the bell is about to ring."

Veronica threw the toilet paper into the wastepaper basket and quickly checked out her reflection in the mirror. "It was nice of you to bring me in here," she said in this formal voice, looking beyond her own reflection to mine.

"No prob," I said breezily. We headed back for Ms. Ferrill's classroom. "So, do you want to meet after school to figure out this project?"

"I'm planning to do two hours of barre work after school," Veronica explained. "Barre work is—"

"Hey, you're in Michigan, not on Mars," I interrupted. "I know what barre work is. You mean you're going to do ballet exercises, right?"

"Right."

"So tomorrow then?" I pressed. I wasn't about to let my social studies grade slip just because Veronica was busy with ballet.

"All right," Veronica agreed. "Would you like to come to my house after school?"

"Yeah, okay, what bus are you on?"

"Oh, Miss Jenkins will pick us up," Veronica said.

I stopped just outside the door to Ferrill's room. "You want to give me a little clue as to who Miss Jenkins is?"

"Our housekeeper," Veronica explained.

"So why is she chauffeuring you around if she's the housekeeper?" I asked.

"Because we haven't hired a chauffeur yet," Veronica replied.

Silly me.

I had never known anyone really, truly rich until I met Veronica.

In Hope there are doctors who make a lot of money, and they live in really big old houses in an area called The Hills. But Veronica was much richer than that. Her mother had inherited millions, she told me, though she never said how. She and her mom lived on the highest hill in The Hills, in a house so big you could get lost in it. And it was only the two of them.

Our house is, frankly, tiny. There's a cramped, little living room, a kitchen with a breakfast nook, a bathroom, and three small bedrooms. Social workers don't make very much money. Also my dad is not very good at financial planning, so we're always short. He has these really big dreams, like that some day he'll invent some gizmo that will make us all really rich, or he'll win the lottery. Sometimes when he spends hours on some new invention that I know will never amount to anything, or when he buys those lottery tickets, I feel really angry, and I get a big lump at the back of my throat. Our house is always so crazy and messy, sometimes I don't even feel like I can breathe there.

So as you can imagine I was perfectly happy to go to Veronica's house—or should I say mansion—every day to work on our project. It was quiet. Serene. And there were fresh flowers everywhere. To me it seemed as if she lived in a movie, this gorgeous ballet dancer dancing around this perfect mansion. Even the snacks at her house were different. Cream cheese with pimento on celery sticks. That one I liked. Something called pate, which tasted like dog food. That one I skipped.

We decided our project on racism would be a play that we'd write together. We made up a story, about a white girl who falls in love with a black guy, and how their families won't let them be together.

"How about if we actually cast the play

with kids in our class," I suggested on the third day we were working together.

"You mean actually put the play on?" Veronica asked.

I nodded. "Ferrill will love that."

"There's only one black student in our social studies class," Veronica pointed out. "Marilee Boston, so she can't play the boy."

"Well, why can't a white person play it?" I asked. "That's more interesting, anyway. And Marilee can play a white bigot. I love that!"

Veronica nodded seriously. "It would be interesting," she allowed.

"Trevor could play the guy," I continued, thinking out loud. "He had the lead in the seventh grade play last year." I fiddled with the little hoop in my left ear. "He's really cute, don't you think?"

"Very," she admitted.

"So, did you have a boyfriend back in New York?"

"Not really," Veronica said. "I was too busy dancing." She played with the end of her hair, which was tied back in a long braid. "Have you known Trevor a long time?"

"Forever," I replied. "He's kind of like my boyfriend."

Okay, so this was a bald-faced lie. I'm not usually a liar. So I guess I just wanted to impress Veronica. So sue me.

"He is?" she asked with surprise.

"Well, not really, but kind of," I said, back-pedaling. "I mean, we hang out and stuff."

"What does that mean?"

"Well, it means we're like . . .on the way to being a couple," I fibbed. "Probably."

"That's nice," she said, a small smile managing to find its way to her lips. "He seems really nice."

"Yeah, so I'll ask him to be in our play tomorrow and everything," I told her, looking at my watch. "I gotta get home. Dad is working late at the hospital, which means I have to make dinner."

"You could stay and eat here," she offered. "We're having duck."

"Gee, we're having Hamburger Helper," I replied, "and if I don't go cook it, my little sister starves. Although maybe if she gets hungry enough she could eat my big brother—that would be great."

Veronica didn't even crack a smile. "I'll ask Miss Jenkins to drive you home."

"So, tomorrow, same time, same place?" I asked her.

"Would after dinner be all right?" Veronica asked me. "I'm planning to work out after school with a ballet tape my teacher made for me."

"Yeah, okay."

"I'll ask Miss Jenkins to pick you up at seven, okay?"

"You got it," I agreed. We walked through the mammoth front hallway, where a crystal chandelier sent prisms of light onto the pristine, white walls. The walls at my house feature peeling paint and crayon scribbles no amount of scrubbing will ever completely erase.

"Hey, does anyone ever call you Roni?" I wondered.

"No."

It figured.

"All ready?" Miss Jenkins said, bustling into the hallway. "Oh, I forgot the keys to the Mercedes—I'll be right back."

Just then the phone rang. "I'll run and get that," Miss Jenkins said.

Veronica frowned. "Everyone knows Mom is at the hospital."

"So, maybe it's for you," I suggested.

"But I don't know anyone here yet. Except you. And you're here."

Veronica can be very literal.

"Veronica, phone call for you," Miss Jenkins said, bustling back into the hallway. "It's a boy."

"A boy?" Veronica echoed, furrowing her brow.

Miss Jenkins nodded. "He said his name is Trevor Wayne."

CHAPTER 4

"My throat hurts," Heidi told me, swishing her long ponytail over the top of the kitchen table.

"It does not," I snapped. "And get your hair off the table."

It was the next day, after school, and I was in the world's worst mood. It turned out that Trevor had called Veronica to invite her to go to the video arcade at the mall with him. His brother, Chris, was driving, and Chris's girlfriend, Donna, was going, too. A double date. Just great.

Veronica told me everything while I stood there in her front hall. Fortunately Miss

Jenkins was waiting in the car, so I didn't have to suffer through my humiliation in front of a witness. I told Veronica that it was fine for her to go out with Trevor, that we weren't exclusive or anything, but she'd already turned him down.

I would give my right arm for a real date with Trevor Wayne, and she had turned him down.

I didn't like her any better for it.

If that wasn't bad enough, at school Trevor would ask me stuff about Veronica, like was there a guy she liked at our school, and did she have a boyfriend back in New York.

"She and I aren't exactly buds," I'd told him. "If you want to ask her out just ask her out."

"Nah, we're just friends," he'd told me.

Sure. Right.

"It hurts when I swallow, Cindy, honest," Heidi said in a little voice. "I'm not making it up."

"Yes, you are," I insisted, trying to finish my algebra homework.

"Could you look at my throat to see if I have cancer?" she asked in a trembly voice.

I sighed and dropped my pencil. "Open up." I looked down her throat. "No cancer."

She scrambled into the chair next to me. "Know what?"

"What?" I mumbled, not looking up from my algebra problem.

"There's a Ferris wheel out by the mall today."

"There is not," I replied, writing down an answer I hoped was correct. Algebra is not my long suit.

"Uh huh," Cindy insisted, swishing her ponytail across the table again just to annoy me. "Lyndsy told me her mom is taking her. There's a merry-go-round and other stuff, too. See?" She handed me a glossy flyer about the fair, a charity event to raise money for Wishful Thinking, an organization that grants wishes to sick kids. My dad had worked with them at Hope Hospital.

"Good," I said, not really paying any attention. I had a ton of homework to finish. Then I planned to work on my one-handed cartwheels and leg-overs for the gymnastics team tryouts, which would be the following week. And after dinner, of course, I was supposed to go back over to Veronica's to work on our play. Maybe I'd get really lucky and Trevor would call her again while I was there. Oh, joy.

"It would be so fun if we could go to the fair," Heidi said.

"Well, we can't," I replied, going on to the next algebra problem.

Clark bounded into the kitchen and immediately stuck his head in the refrigerator. "There's nothing to eat in this house," he complained. Then he turned to me. "How come there's nothing to eat?"

"But if we could just go for a little while—" Heidi wheedled, pulling on the sleeve of my sweatshirt.

"You two are driving me nuts!" I yelled, jumping up from the table. "I'm going to my room."

"It's my room, too," Heidi said in a small voice, but I did my best to ignore her.

Why was everything my responsibility? Why couldn't I just be a kid like everyone else? I tried to remember what it had been like when Mom was still alive, back when no one expected me to act like I was the parent. But the memories of Mom were fading. Someday they might be gone completely.

I tried not to think about that too much.

About a half hour later I was finishing my algebra when there was a tiny knock at the door.

"What?" I yelled.

The door swung open. Heidi stood there, tears streaked across her face. "Are you mad at me?" she asked.

"Come here," I said, and held my arms open to her. I really loved Heidi, and she was just a little girl. A little girl without a mother.

I hugged her close and felt terrible that I'd been so mean to her. "It's okay about the fair," she told me in a serious voice.

"It is?"

She nodded solemnly. "It's because we don't have money to go, right? That's okay. I know we don't have any money."

"Hey, Cin, I'm taking Melanie to the fair out at the mall," Clark called from the kitchen. "I'm taking five bucks for gas from the can."

"The can" is the coffee tin we keep in the kitchen with household money in it. There's not usually very much money in there, and it wasn't supposed to go toward Clark's dates with his stupid girlfriend. The only reason the car was home was because Dad had ridden his bike to the hospital that morning.

I ran into the hallway and caught Clark before he got out the door. "We're going with you," I told him.

"Hurrah!" Heidi yelled, bouncing on my bed with glee.

"Come on," Clark said. "It's a date—"

"Don't worry, we won't hang out with you," I told him, reaching for my purse. "We don't want to be seen with you any more than you want to be seen with us."

"Yeah," Heidi agreed, reaching for my hand. "We're having our own date."

Our own date. I sighed. A date with my little sister might be as close to a real date as I would ever get.

"I want to go on the merry-go-round again!" Heidi squealed happily. "I want the horse with the pink saddle!"

"Okay," I agreed, and we got back in line again.

"I'm having the best time ever," Heidi told me, a huge grin on her face. "Can we get another cotton candy?"

"No, it'll spoil your dinner," I said without thinking. Then I caught myself. Had I really said that? I sounded like I was someone's mother.

Yuck.

"Noooooo, that girl is getting on my horsie!" Heidi yelled, pointing toward a red-haired little girl who was scrambling onto Heidi's favorite pony. "Make her get off!"

"I can't," I said patiently, even though I didn't feel very patient.

"But it's my horse!" Heidi protested.

"You know that's not true," I said in a low voice. We reached the front of the line and I handed a bored-looking guy with pimples two tickets.

"That girl is on my horse!" Heidi told the guy.

"So find another horse," he said in a tired voice, taking the next person's ticket.

"It isn't fair," Heidi mumbled, but she ran over to a purple horse and waited for me to help her up.

The merry-go-round started and Heidi forgot all about how upset she was over not getting to ride on the pink horse. I had to smile, watching her happy face. She really was a cute kid, and little things could make her so happy.

"When we get off of here I'll get you another cotton candy!" I called to her over the music.

"Really?" she asked, joy spreading across her face.

"Sure," I told her. So what that I had already spent five dollars on ride tickets and junk food. So what that we didn't have any groceries in the house. I wanted to get my little sister another cotton candy, and I didn't want to sound like any stupid grown-up or worry about grown-up things.

We got off the merry-go-round and then I bought Heidi the hugest multicolored cotton candy you ever saw. The fair was fun. There was great music playing and everyone was running around having a blast. I felt so good I did a double cartwheel, and Heidi clapped and jumped up and down. Of course it would have been more fun if Jennifer had been with me—maybe we would have found some guys to flirt with—but still I found myself in a happy mood.

That is, until I saw *them.*

Trevor and Veronica. Together. Laughing and walking right toward us. How could they? She was supposed to be home working on her ballet, and he was supposed to be . . . I didn't know. Anywhere except at that fair with that girl.

"Let's go on the Ferris wheel," I said to Heidi, and quickly pulled her in the opposite direction from Trevor and Veronica.

"It's too big," Heidi protested, dragging behind me.

"No, it isn't," I insisted. "You'll love it." We got in line and I snuck a look around. Good. Trevor and Veronica hadn't seen me. They were standing in front of a booth where some fat guy was guessing people's weights.

"I don't wanna go," Heidi said, biting her lower lip. "I'm scared."

"Don't be such a baby," I replied without thinking, my eyes still peeled to the sight of Trevor and Veronica. Hadn't she told me she wouldn't go out with him? What a liar! And hadn't he told me they were just friends? They were *both* liars!

"I have to go to the bathroom," Heidi whined, pulling on my hand.

"You can hold it," I told her absent-mindedly, my eyes still glued to Veronica and Trevor. Now they were laughing and walking toward us. We were almost to the front of the line.

"But—"

"Two please," I told the ticket guy, and I half-dragged my little sister toward the Ferris wheel.

"Are you sure it's not scary?" Heidi asked me.

"Positive," I assured her, as the guy closed the metal bar in front of us.

"No leaning against the bar," he told us. "No standing up in the car."

Now Trevor and Veronica were walking right by the Ferris wheel. I prayed they wouldn't turn in our direction.

Our cart moved off the platform so the last cart could be filled. We swung a few feet off the ground.

"I don't like it when it swings," Heidi said tremulously.

"It's perfectly safe, sweetie," I told her, still not paying any attention to her. Good. They were walking by. They hadn't seen me.

The music began and the Ferris wheel took off. We swooped into the air until Trevor and Veronica were little tiny ants on the ground.

"We're so high in the sky!" Heidi yelled joyously. "We're the highest anyone's ever been in the world!"

"I told you it would be fun," I said, finally tearing my eyes away from the teeny tiny images of Trevor and Veronica down there on the ground. As we swooped around back to the ground I looked for them again, but I couldn't find them. Then we went back up into the air, and I decided I was going to enjoy the ride and not think about them at all.

"We're higher than an airplane, right?" Heidi cried. She took a bite of her cotton candy. "This is the most fun I ever had!"

We swooped around and around, the crisp fall air whooshing into our faces. I really started having a great time. But on the next pass to the ground I saw Veronica and Trevor again. They were in line, waiting to get on the Ferris wheel. Now there was no way I could possibly sneak away without seeing them. What was I going to do?

"I'm not scared, I'm not scared, I'm fly-y-y-ing!" Heidi yelled into the wind. She bounced around joyfully, pretending she was a bird.

"Sit back," I told her sharply. "You can't play around in here."

"I'm fly-y-ying!" she yelled again, as we swooped back up the arc of the Ferris wheel.

My eyes were still on Veronica and Trevor when Heidi somehow let go of her cotton candy. Without thinking she jumped up to catch it, and that's when it happened.

The safety bar gave way.

Heidi screamed my name. I'll remember that scream, that moment, for as long as I live.

I reached out for her, just touching the edge of her red and white sweatshirt, but it all happened so fast, and her little body was beyond my grasp, as Heidi flew through the air and hurtled toward the earth.

CHAPTER 5

It was all my fault.

That was what kept repeating over and over in my head.

After Heidi fell off the Ferris wheel, everything happened so quickly that it was all a blur—Heidi lying motionless on the ground, people standing around speaking in these horrible hushed voices, the sound of the sirens, then paramedics loading Heidi into the back of the ambulance. Somehow Clark was there, and we both got into the ambulance with the paramedics.

Now we were sitting with Dad outside of intensive care at Hope Hospital, waiting to hear whether Heidi would live or die.

"I wish Jennifer was here," I whispered out loud to no one in particular.

Dad kept pacing back and forth, back and forth, running his hands over and over through his long hair.

"Man, I can't take it if she dies," Clark said. "I can't handle it."

"She isn't going to die," Dad said, overhearing Clark. "She can't die."

I knew he was wrong, though. Once I thought Mom couldn't possibly die, and she did. Which meant that anyone could die. At any time.

And it would be all my fault.

"Mr. Winters?" A policeman stood in front of my father, looking at him expectantly.

"Yes," my dad said.

"My name is Sergeant Moreno. I need to fill out an accident report, sir. If you could tell me what happened—"

"I wasn't there," Dad replied. He looked over at me.

"I was with my sister," I said in a small voice.

The policeman walked over to me. "Could you tell me what happened?" He stood with his pen poised over a piece of paper.

"She . . . she just leaned forward," I said, gulping hard. "She wanted to get her cotton candy. And the . . . the bar that's supposed to hold you in didn't catch her, and then . . ." Tears began to fall down my cheeks. I felt as if it was the end of the world. "I should have been able to stop her!" I yelled. "I tried to reach her, but I was too late!"

Dad came over to me and put his arms around me. I buried my face in his chest, sobbing hard. Dad turned to the policeman. "Could this wait, please?"

"It's best to do it while the memory is fresh in your daughter's mind, sir," the policeman said. "Obviously there's the possibility of a major lawsuit here against the—"

"I don't care about that!" Dad yelled. Dad never yells. "Just leave us alone right now!"

The cop vanished.

"Daddy, it was all my fault!" I sobbed.

"No, sweetheart," Dad managed to say.

"Yes, it is," I insisted. "I'll never forgive myself if she—"

"She won't," Dad said.

"Right," Clark agreed, sitting down next to me. His face was white and he looked as scared as I felt. "She's going to be okay. She has to be okay."

It was only a short while, but it felt like we waited forever in that waiting room.

Nurses and doctors who knew my dad kept coming by to offer their prayers and good wishes. Clark's girlfriend came over with Clark's best friend, Alex. I guess he went over to the fair and picked her up.

But as for me, I was all alone. There was no Jennifer there to sit by my side. There was no one at all.

And then Veronica walked in the door. With Trevor.

"What are you doing here?" I said, staring up at them.

"We came to see you," Veronica said, sitting down next to me. "We were at the fair . . ."

"Look, I don't want you here," I said in a strained voice. Somehow seeing Veronica and Trevor made me feel even more guilty. If I hadn't been so busy looking at them, worrying they'd see me, worrying that I'd get caught in my lie about being his girlfriend, this might never have happened.

"Cin, I'm really sorry," Trevor said, putting his hand on my shoulder.

"Why should *you* be sorry?" I said bitterly, shaking his hand away. "*You* didn't do anything wrong. I did."

"You didn't do anything, either," Trevor insisted. "The safety bar was broken, that's what everyone said at the fair."

"Just leave me alone," I told him. "Just go away!"

He looked over at Veronica, but she shook her head no. "I'm staying," she told him. "I'll call Miss Jenkins and get a ride home later."

"I could stay, too," Trevor offered.

"Don't do me any favors," I snapped, and turned my face away from him.

Trevor shuffled around, his hands in the pockets of his jeans.

"Trev?" his brother Chris called from the doorway. "You staying or what?"

"You really want me to go?" Trevor asked me.

"Yes," I said. "I really do."

"Okay, then," he finally said. "I . . . I'll call you." He walked away.

"Like I said, you can go, too," I told Veronica. "I don't even know why you're here. It's not like we're really friends."

Veronica didn't react to what I'd said. She just sat there, next to me.

Finally, a doctor came out of the swinging doors. He walked over to Dad. I dug the nails of my right hand into the flesh of my left hand until painful crescents of red blood dotted my skin. It felt good to hurt.

Please, I prayed silently. *Please . . .*

"Mr. Winters?"

"Yes?"

"I'm Dr. Reuben."

"My daughter—?"

"She's alive," Dr. Reuben replied. "There are multiple fractures of both legs and one of her lungs has collapsed. We're not certain yet about the extent of the internal damage. It appears that there is internal bleeding in the skull, possibly a fracture. We need your permission to operate to stop it."

"Is the surgery dangerous?" my father asked in a low voice.

"It could be," Dr. Reuben admitted. "But if we don't go in, she could die."

Dad looked at the doctor hard. "What would you do if it was your five-year-old daughter?" he asked.

"I'd operate," Dr. Reuben said without a hesitation.

Dad just stood there, staring out at nothing. Somehow I knew he was thinking about Mom. He ran his shaking fingers across his face. Everyone stood there, staring at him, waiting for him to make a decision.

That's when Veronica stood up and walked over to Dr. Reuben and Dad.

"Excuse me," she said. "I'm Veronica Langley. My mother is Doctor Patricia Langley, the new head of pediatric surgery."

"Yes?" Dr. Reuben acknowledged impatiently.

"If you don't mind, doctor, I'd like my mother consulted on this," Veronica said smoothly.

"Look, Miss Langley, time is of the essence here—" Dr. Reuben began in a cold voice.

"Could we page my mother, stat, please?" Veronica said in a firm voice.

I'd been around the hospital enough to know that "stat" meant immediately.

Dr. Reuben threw up his hands and strode over to the nurses' station, where a page went out over the intercom for Dr. Langley.

Within two minutes, a woman who looked just like Veronica, only older, practically ran into the room. Dr. Reuben spoke with her in a low voice. She listened and nodded.

Veronica put her hand on her mother's

arm. "She's my friend's little sister," she told her mother. "Please, Mom, if Heidi has to have the surgery, do it yourself."

"Dr. Reuben is a very good surgeon, Veronica," Dr. Langley told her daughter.

"I'm sure he is," Veronica agreed. "But he isn't you."

Dr. Langley spoke quickly with Dr. Reuben, who nodded and walked away. Then she turned to Dad. "Mr. Winters?"

"Yes."

"I'm Doctor Langley, head of pediatric surgery. I'm also Veronica's mother."

"Yes," Dad said dully.

"I'm going to go check on your daughter. From what Dr. Reuben told me it sounds as if Heidi needs this surgery right away. I'll check her and give you my opinion."

Dad nodded. "Thank you."

"It would help if you could sign the consent form now, Mr. Winters," Dr. Langley said. "Then if I feel Heidi needs the surgery I can begin immediately."

"You'll do the surgery yourself?" Dad asked her.

"She will," Veronica said, answering for her mom. "She won't let Heidi die."

Dr. Langley looked at her daughter. "I wish I could make that guarantee, but I can't. I will tell you that I will do my very best."

We sat there for hours. I never said anything to Veronica. Once she got me a Coke, and once she brought all of us sandwiches from the cafeteria. I didn't eat a bite. How could I eat, how could I drink, when I didn't know if Heidi was even going to be alive the next day? When I didn't know if she was even alive that very minute?

Every time I looked at Veronica I felt worse. Everything was so mixed up in my head. Was she being nice to me because she felt bad that she had gone out with Trevor, when I'd lied and told her he was my boyfriend? Did she just feel sorry for me?

Part of me wished she'd just leave, but another part of me was glad that someone cared enough about me to sit there with me. At least she didn't say anything stupid. People said stupid things to me when Mom was dying, like that she was strong so she'd pull through, like that she wasn't suffering. Both were lies. Big, fat, stupid lies.

It was really late when Dr. Langley finally came through the double doors, pulling off her surgical mask as she walked toward Dad. She looked exhausted. Everyone jumped up—Dad, Clark, Alex, Melanie, me, and Veronica. Without even thinking about it I reached out and grabbed Veronica's hand. We all stood there, staring at Dr. Langley, wanting to know and not wanting to know at the same time.

"I've just finished surgery," Dr. Langley began.

"Yes?" Dad asked, his hands clenched into two fists.

Dr. Langley hesitated. Just the way the doctor had hesitated when he came out of Mom's room that last time.

And that was when I knew.

It had to be really, really bad.

CHAPTER 6

Please, no, I couldn't listen to her say the words. I would run away, far away to some place where no one I loved ever died and—

". . . touch and go for a while, but Heidi made it through the surgery," Dr. Langley was saying.

"Thank you! Thank you so much!" Dad cried. He hugged her, then he hugged me and Clark.

"You mean she's okay?" I asked when Dad stopped smothering me. "Heidi is okay?"

"I told you my mother wouldn't let Heidi die," Veronica said simply.

"But . . . but you looked so serious when you came out here—" I began.

"I can't tell any of you that Heidi is completely out of the woods," Dr. Langley said cautiously. "The next twenty-four hours will tell us a lot. But her vital signs are strong. I think she'll make it."

"I can't thank you enough," Dad said. There were tears in his eyes.

"There's no need to thank me," Dr. Langley told him briskly. "I just did my job. You do understand that even if things go very well, Heidi will need a great deal of care and rehabilitation. She'll certainly need further surgery on her legs. She's going to be in the hospital for a long time."

"Anything," Dad said, "as long as she's okay. As long as my little girl lives. Can I see her?"

"She's deeply under the anesthetic now," Dr. Langley said. "But I'll have the nurse call you as soon as Heidi begins to come out of it."

"If I could just wait by her bed?" Dad asked hopefully.

"All right," Dr. Langley agreed reluctantly. "But don't interfere in any way. She's down that hall in the intensive care unit, in recovery room three."

"Thank you for saving my sister," I told Veronica's mom.

"Yeah, thanks," Clark added, his eyes shining with tears.

"As I said, it's my job," Dr. Langley said. "I'm glad things turned out well. Now, if you'll excuse me, please."

"Your mother is a wonderful doctor," I told Veronica fervently as I watched Dr. Langley walk away.

"Yes, she is," Veronica agreed, looking after her mother. "If only she was a wonderful mother."

It was a very strange thing to say, but I was much too involved in my own problems right at that moment to care much about Veronica's.

Hope is such a small town that by the next day everyone at school knew what had happened to my sister. A lot of people were talking about how we should sue the people who did the fair, or the makers of the Ferris wheel. Dad had a really long talk with our lawyer and I had to answer a million questions for the police report. Footage from the accident was even on the news—someone at the fair had had a video camera—and they sold the footage to the nearest network television affiliate. I couldn't bare to watch it.

I was a celebrity. Kids were really nice to me. They kept coming up to me at school and telling me how sorry they were, asking me if they could do anything to help. The whole thing made me kind of sick. I mean, Dawn McKnight and Krystal Franklin normally didn't give me the time of day. Now they were hanging all over me like we were best friends.

The girls from my gymnastics team sent flowers and stuffed animals to Heidi at the hospital, and that was nice, but Jennifer and I had always hung out together so much that I'd never gotten to be really good friends with any of them. In fact, the only one I really wanted to talk to was Jennifer. Every time I called her in San Francisco to tell her what had happened, I got a busy signal. I figured she'd made so many new friends that she was on the phone with them all the time, and she'd probably totally forgotten about me.

I did my best to ignore Trevor and Veronica. Every time I saw them, they were together. And every time either one of them wanted to talk to me, I just walked away.

I'm not telling you this was mature on my part, I'm just telling you the way it was.

Three days after Heidi's accident I was in a good mood, since when I had called the hospital at lunchtime the nurse told me Heidi had improved enough to be transferred into the regular pediatric unit. Heidi hates being alone—I knew it would make her happy to be with a lot of other kids.

"Hey, Winters," Trevor said as he sidled up next to me in the hall after fifth period. "How's the kid?"

"Better," I reported. "She's moving to a regular room in the kids' wing today."

"Hey, great!" Trevor exclaimed. "You going over there after school?"

"Yeah." I started to walk away from him, per usual.

"So, I'll go with you," Trevor offered, catching up to me.

"No, thanks," I said. It's what I told him every day.

He stopped walking and stared at me. "Could you just stop and talk to me for a second?"

"I'm kind of in a hurry—"

"Look, Cin, what's the deal?"

"No deal," I replied, "I'm just busy."

"So why don't you want me to come with you to visit Heidi?"

"I just don't need you along, okay?"

"I thought we were supposed to be friends," Trevor reminded me. "And I really like Heidi," Trevor said. "I mean, I'd really like to go with you."

"Well, I can't physically stop you from going to the hospital, if that's what you want to do," I said nastily, brushing some hair out of my eyes.

"Why are you being such a witch?" Trevor asked. "I really want to know what I did that's ticking you off so much."

The bell rang for fifth period and I hurried away from him without answering. What could I possibly say, anyway? I hate you for being my friend instead of my boyfriend? I hate that you like Veronica instead of me? I hate myself for caring?

No. I really couldn't say anything at all.

"I brought you Raggedy Ann," I told Heidi, laying my favorite doll in her arms.

"Thanks," Heidi said in a whispery voice. Her head was shaved and wrapped in bandages, with drains that led down to two plastic bulbs hanging off of her. The bulbs were filled up with blood and fluid from her brain. That made me feel kind of sick and I looked quickly down at her legs.

Both of them were in casts all the way up to her waist. And still, she managed to smile for me.

"Want some juice, sweetie pie?" Dad asked her, reaching for the apple juice. Heidi slurped a little through the straw.

"Thanks, Daddy," she whispered, then she closed her eyes. She was still heavily medicated, and she slept a lot.

I looked around the small room, which was painted pink and filled with flowers. On one wall there was a mural of Disney characters. A poster on the door showed three kittens falling off a clothes line, and it read "HANG IN THERE."

I walked over to the window and looked outside. Out on the lawn two kids in wheelchairs were laughing and throwing popcorn at each other. The nurse who was with them didn't seem to mind. In fact, she joined right in.

How soon would it be before Heidi was out there throwing popcorn with them? How soon would it be before Heidi laughed again?

"What's wrong with her?" A skinny, little African-American boy who looked about ten stood in the doorway. The initial *J* was shaved into his haircut. He balanced himself on crutches.

I looked down. One of his legs ended just above the knee.

"I don't have a leg anymore," he told me, as he hopped into the room on his crutches.

"I can see that," I replied, since I didn't know what else to say.

"I lost it in a gang war," the little boy added.

My father laughed.

"A big gang war," the boy continued. "I have my own gang. Another dude shot off my leg. Then I iced him."

"Jerome has a great imagination," Dad told me. "Jerome Winslow, this is my daughter, Cindy Winters."

"I know your dad 'cuz he hangs out with us," Jerome said. "He's teaching me to juggle."

"Yeah, he's a great juggler," I agreed.

"So who is the girl with all the bandages?" Jerome asked.

"My other daughter," Dad said, tenderly straightening Heidi's covers. "Her name is Heidi."

"She looks sick," Jerome decided. "So now

that your own daughter is in here, does that mean you won't have time to hang with the rest of us anymore?" Jerome asked Dad.

"I'll have time," he assured Jerome. "I promise."

"You probably only hang with us because it's your job and you'd get fired if you didn't," Jerome said matter-of-factly. "So what happened to your daughter?"

"She was in a bad accident," Dad explained. "She fell out of a Ferris wheel."

"For real?" Jerome asked, his eyes lighting up. "Does she still have both her legs underneath those casts?"

"There you are!" a little girl cried, toddling over to us. "Jerome, you said you were gonna watch cartoons with me."

She was about four, and her face was all round and puffy. She was totally bald, and she had a pink ribbon wrapped around her head.

A needle was in her right arm, attached to a long thin piece of tubing so medication could drip into her arm. She wheeled a pole where the medicine hung in a bag over her head.

"I'm busy now," Jerome told her. He turned back to Dad. "You must be real mad at the company that makes that Ferris wheel, right?"

"I'm not really thinking about that right now," Dad told Jerome.

"Well, you should sue them for ten million dollars," Jerome said. "That's what I'd do. You want me to get my dad to sue them? He's a lawyer."

"I know," Dad said with a small smile.

"Or I could get my gang to off the head of that company," Jerome offered. "My gang is very, very bad. Dangerous."

"No, thanks," Dad replied.

The little girl snuggled up to my father, careful not to disturb the needle in her arm. "Hi, Dr. Dan," she said. "Wanna watch cartoons?" she asked hopefully.

"Not right now, Brianna," Dad told her. "These are my daughters, Cindy and Heidi."

"Your little girl is sick?" Brianna asked, looking concerned.

"Yes, but she's getting better," Dad told her. "I bet when she feels better she'll watch TV with you. She loves cartoons."

"There you are!" a nurse said, fluttering into the room. She had long blond hair held back by a pale blue ribbon, and she seemed to sort of float along on her tippy toes. There were three—count 'em, three—smiley face buttons of different colors pinned to her uniform, and a little lace handkerchief peeked out of her pocket.

"I thought I had you parked in front of the TV," she said to the little girl.

"I'm visiting," Brianna said with dignity. "Dr. Dan's little girl is sick," she added.

"I know, sweetie," the nurse said softly. "But we have magic fairy dust here, and I'm going to sprinkle it on Dr. Dan's little girl to help her get well!"

Magic fairy dust?

The nurse reached into her pocket and pulled something out in her fist, then she opened her hand and blew on it. There was nothing there.

"I didn't see anything," Brianna said.

"That's the magic part!" the nurse chirped. She turned to my father and batted her eyelashes. "How are you doing, Dan?"

There was something about the way she said "Dan" I didn't like. Something intimate, like her voice was kissing him, and we're not talking about a peck on the cheek.

"Fine," Dad replied. "This is my daughter, Cindy. Cindy, this is Rachel Dander, a friend of mine."

A "friend"? How close a "friend"?

"Hi," I said.

"It's super to finally meet you," Rachel gushed. "I've heard so much about you."

I shot Dad a look. When had she heard so much about me and why?

"Rachel and I work together," Dad explained, but he sounded nervous when he said it.

"Well, if there's anything I can do, anything at all . . ." Rachel let the rest of her sentence trail away into thin air. "Well, Brianna and I will be going, then. You coming, Jerome?"

"I got business here, woman," Jerome said gruffly.

"Is he okay in here with you?" Rachel asked Dad.

"Sure," Dad said. "For a little while."

"Me and Dr. Dan are homies," Jerome explained.

"Let's go play Barbies," Brianna suggested to Rachel, taking her hand.

"Bye," Rachel said. "If you need anything . . ."

Once again she didn't finish her sentence. She just waved and left.

"Brianna—that little girl that was just in here—she's got cancer," Jerome informed me, matter-of-factly. "Leukemia. She's gonna die."

"Why do you say that?" Dad asked him.

Jerome shrugged. "'Cuz it's true. You play chess?" he asked me.

"Not very well," I admitted.

"Good, then we'll play for money," Jerome said. "You wanna play now?"

"No," I said, smiling in spite of myself.

Heidi opened her eyes. "Daddy?"

"I'm right here, honey," he said, stroking her forehead.

"I was having a dream," Heidi said sleepily, and then she closed her eyes again.

"So, how old are you?" Jerome asked me, shifting around on his crutches.

"Thirteen."

"I'm ten," Jerome said. "But my girlfriend is fourteen. She's in a gang, too. You wanna go out some time?"

"Jerome, maybe you should go hang out someplace else right now," Dad told him. "Okay?"

"Cool with me, homie," Jerome agreed with a shrug. He quickly maneuvered to the door on his crutches, then he looked back at me. "I'll take you to the movies. Something R-rated. I got my own car."

"Weird kid," I said when Jerome was out of the room. "So how come everyone calls you Dr. Dan when you're not a doctor?"

"The kids made that up," Dad said. "I wanted them to just call me Dan, but I do this funny doctor imitation that cracks them up, so they started calling me Dr. Dan, and it just stuck."

"You never even told me that," I said. It didn't seem right to me that my dad had this whole secret life at the hospital that I didn't even know about.

"That's 'cause you call me dad," he said with a grin.

"So what's with that kid, Jerome?" I asked.

"He's a great kid," Dad said. "Really smart. He just pretends to be tough and streetwise. Actually his parents are really rich and he gets straight A's at a private school."

"No kidding," I marveled. "So what happened to his leg?"

"He has bone cancer," Dad said. "He's been here for a long time."

Something turned over in my stomach. "That's terrible! And that bald little girl, Brianna? Jerome said she had cancer."

"Leukemia," Dad said. "Cancer of the blood. She's bald and puffed up from the chemotherapy."

I shivered, even though it was warm in

the room. Life was just so bizarre. Heidi was always so afraid she had cancer, and now she was in a place with kids who really *did* have it.

"So are they going to be okay?" I asked.

Dad gave me a lopsided smile. "When someone asks me that, I always say yes."

"That's kind of dumb, Dad."

"Nah," Dad said, looking down at Heidi. "Kids can take a lot. The parents usually fall apart long before the kid does."

"But some kids with cancer . . . well, they die, don't they?" I asked.

Like mom, I was thinking.

"Hope has one of the highest remission rates for kids with cancer in the country," Dad said.

"But some of them still die," I insisted. "I know they do."

"Hey, you wanna go get some ice cream or something?" Dad asked me. "There's always ice cream in the kids' lounge."

"Why won't you answer my question?"

"The kids here named it the NAAH Club— it stands for No Adults Allowed Here. The doctors aren't even allowed to come in there to—"

"I hate it when you change the subject like that, Dad—"

"We'll talk about it later, okay?" He stood up and ruffled my hair, which is another thing I hate. "Let's go get some ice cream. Then I'll show you around."

"Sure," I said with a sigh, giving in to Dad, per usual.

Because as sure as I knew that Heidi's accident was all my fault, I knew that for Dad "later" would never come.

CHAPTER 7

"Come on, I'll show you the teen wing," Dad said.

He'd just finished walking me through pediatrics. I had met a ton of kids, and they all called my dad Dr. Dan. My head was reeling. About a third of them were bald from chemotherapy, four kids were in wheelchairs, one boy lay on his stomach on a stretcher and could only move his head.

"This place is so depressing," I muttered, as we went through a door marked "Foxx Wing."

"You think so?" Dad asked.

"Who wouldn't?" I watched a bald kid with a patch over one eye take a drink from a drinking fountain.

"I guess I don't see it that way," Dad said. "Well, here we are, the Foxes Den. Pretty fab, huh?"

"Wow," was all I could manage. We were standing in a huge room that looked like something out of a teen fantasy. On one wall was a giant TV screen. At the moment two teenage girls were watching a soap opera. Next to that was a box full of video-tapes. Two computers and three old pinball machines lined another wall.

A sign in the corner read "Return CDs Here," and there was a state-of-the-art CD player next to it. An old-fashioned jukebox with blue and pink neon was right next to that. Then there was a game area, with chess, checkers, Monopoly, Risk, every game you could think of.

Over in another corner there was art stuff—an easel, a potter's wheel, pastels, and pads of paper. Standing at the easel painting was a guy who looked like he was about fourteen or fifteen. He was medium height and really thin. He wore baggy jeans and a sweatshirt with Kurt Cobain's picture on it. His blond hair fell over one eye and he had an intense, serious look on his face. He wasn't as cute as Trevor, but there was something—I don't know—sensitive about his face.

I looked around the room some more. The walls were lined with posters for alternative bands. There was a bookshelf full of books. A guy and a girl sat reading on two huge, overstuffed couches.

"It sure doesn't seem like we're in a hospital," I marveled to Dad. "The little kids' lounge doesn't look anything like this."

"That's because of Jeremy Foxx," Dad said.

"Jeremy Foxx from *Foxxy and Friends?*" I asked incredulously. Jeremy Foxx was a stand-up comic who now had his own sitcom, about a bunch of struggling actors in New York City who all lived in the same apartment building. It was the most popular show on TV.

"Yep," Dad said. "Jeremy's little sister, Angie, was here at Hope for a long time when she was fourteen."

"How come I never knew that?" I asked.

"You were only ten then," Dad explained. "Besides, Jeremy wasn't famous yet. Anyway, she had a very rare and deadly form of leukemia—"

"How did she end up at Hope?" I interrupted.

"This hospital is famous for its work with certain childhood diseases," Dad explained. "We get kids here from all over the world."

"I didn't know that," I marveled. The boy at the easel stepped back from what he was painting and looked at it carefully. I wondered what color eyes he had. I wondered why he was in a hospital.

"When Jeremy's sister got here she was in really bad shape," Dad continued. "But we were able to put her into a complete remission. Today she's cancer-free."

"That's terrific!" I exclaimed.

Dad nodded. "Jeremy was so grateful that when he hit it big he donated a lot of money to the hospital, and he stipulated that part of the money be used for a really great teen lounge."

"It should have been in the news or something," I said, looking at the twenty-foot figures kissing on the giant TV screen.

"It was," Dad said with a laugh. "You just don't pay any attention to what's in the paper."

"I stink," the boy at the easel said with disgust, and he threw his paintbrush down.

"Who is that?" I asked Dad.

"I don't know," Dad said. "I only work in pediatrics—with the little kids. Anyone over the age of eleven or twelve who gets admitted comes over here instead."

"Oh my gosh, you guys, you have to see this!" A cute, plump Asian-looking girl with a shiny, bouncy black bob haircut ran over to the two girls watching TV, waving a small pad of paper in their faces.

"Not now, Tina, we're watching this!" the skinny girl with the red hair whined.

"We have to find out if Tiffany is really Bronson's love child," the other girl explained, her eyes glued to the soap opera.

"This is better than any soap, I swear," Tina insisted. "Guess what Virgin-for-Life Head Nurse Virginia Overton was doodling on a prescription pad at the nurses' station?"

"What?" the redhead asked, since a commercial had just come on.

"Mrs. Virginia Maxwell! Mrs. Albert Maxwell! Mrs. Dr. Albert Maxwell! Then she drew little hearts all over the place!" Tina hooted, waving the pad of paper around. "I just casually happened to look over at it when she got called into Marilyn's room.

And there it was! She's writing her name with his, pretending they're married!"

"But Dr. Maxwell is already married!" the redhead said.

"Well, duh," the other girl snorted.

"I told you, it's like a real-life soap opera!" Tina exclaimed. "I knew she was in love with Dr. Maxwell! I just knew it!"

"Lemme see that!" the redhead cried, reaching for the piece of paper. "This is hilarious! I thought she was, like, a nun or something!"

"Tina Wu, did you steal the pad I was writing on?" asked a deep voice from the doorway.

Standing there was a woman who was at least six feet tall and had to weigh at least two hundred pounds. She looked like something from the Wide World of Wrestling.

"I didn't steal it . . . exactly," Tina said, biting her lip to keep from laughing. "I did sort of . . . borrow it."

"Well, you can just sort of return it this instant," the huge woman bellowed, holding out her hand.

Tina walked over to her, her head down (but I could see her shoulders were shaking with laughter), and put the pad in the woman's hand.

"Don't ever do that again," the nurse said, her face turning bright red. Then she turned on her heel and marched out.

"Honey, I want to go check on Heidi," Dad said. "You want to stay here?"

"I'll come with you," I said, though I was still watching the girl named Tina, who was falling all over herself laughing.

"No, stay here for a little while," Dad suggested. "Heidi's probably still asleep. I'll come back and get you and I'll give you the rest of the tour."

I wandered over to the CDs and looked at the titles, while behind me Tina was still chattering away about Virginia.

"Shut up, Tina! The show is back on," one girl said irritably.

"You guys, real-life is better than that show," Tina told them, but she sounded good-natured about it. The next thing I knew she was standing next to me. "Hi, who are you?"

"Cindy Winters," I replied.

"I'm Tina Wu," she said easily. "What are you in for?"

She was about three inches taller than me and she had a friendly smile. I noticed she had on mascara and lip gloss. No one I know wears make-up—at least not for every day. She was wearing a cute red corduroy miniskirt with suspenders.

"I'm just visiting," I explained. "My little sister had an accident—"

"Hey, I recognize you!" she cried, snapping her fingers. "From the news! Your sister fell out of that Ferris wheel, right? That was so terrible! Is she okay?"

"She's going to be. I hope." I looked over at the blond-haired guy at the easel. He had put up a new piece of paper, and he was painting with long, looping strokes.

"That's Brad Kennedy," she told me. "Isn't he darling?"

"He's okay," I said. "Is he a patient here?"

She nodded. "I don't know what he's got, though. He just came in yesterday. Usually I know everything about everyone. He's been in here painting for hours. I love artistic guys, don't you?"

I shrugged and looked her over carefully. "You don't seem very . . . sick," I ventured.

"I'm having a good day," she said cheerfully. "It's amazing what the right drugs can do for a girl. I've got lupus—you've probably never heard of it."

"Right," I agreed.

She blew on her bangs to get them out of her eyes. "It's an autoimmune disease," she explained. "You probably don't know what that is, either."

"Right again."

"That's okay, I wouldn't know what it was either if I didn't have it," she said with a grin. "Well, see, it's this disease where your body's immune system—that's what fights off diseases—your immune system gets these false signals. So it thinks that your internal organs and your joints are, like, disease."

"So what happens?" I asked, sitting down on a carved chair with a thick black cushion.

"Well, sometimes I get really sick," Tina explained, sitting across from me. "Like I run fevers, and all my joints hurt, and sometimes I have problems with my heart or my lungs or my kidneys. This time I had depressed platelets in my blood—big fun."

"What's that?"

"It means I was bleeding too easily," she explained. "And I was exhausted—I could hardly drag myself into the garage for school!"

"You go to school in a garage?" I asked in fascination.

"Home schooling," she said. "Or in my case, garage-schooling. My mom has a teaching degree and—hey, want to go talk to Brad? He stopped painting."

I looked over at Brad. He was putting his paints away in a white metal box.

"How do you know his name?" I wondered.

"I asked him," she said with a laugh. "I'm not shy."

"I can see that," I replied. "So why didn't you just ask him what's wrong with him?"

"I did!" she assured me. "He just didn't tell me!" She stood up. "Let's go ask him together!"

"No!" I hissed. "I can't just walk up to a boy and—"

But I never got to finish my sentence, because right at that moment who but Veronica Langley walked into the Foxes Den. She walked right over to Brad Kennedy.

And she gave him a big hug.

CHAPTER 8

"Lucky her, whoever she is," Tina said, watching Veronica and Brad hugging across the room. "I guess that's his girlfriend."

"No," I said. "Not unless she's got two boyfriends, anyway."

"How do you know?" Tina asked.

"Because she's going out with Trevor Wayne, this other guy I know. We used to be really good buds, but—it's a long story."

"So who is she?" Tina asked. "She's absolutely gorgeous and her hair is perfect. She looks like a model."

"Her name is Veronica Langley," I reported, still watching Veronica and Brad, who had stopped hugging but were still holding hands, having some kind of intense conversation. "She just moved to Hope. Her mom is the new head of pediatrics here."

"So how did she and Brad get together so fast?" Tina wondered.

I shrugged morosely. "Maybe she's just some kind of guy-magnet."

"My cousin Alexa is like that," Tina said, nodding knowingly. "She's at least twenty pounds overweight and her front teeth are crooked, but guys just flock around her all the time."

"What's her secret?" I asked.

Tina shrugged. "I asked her once. She said it was because she thinks she's hot stuff. She says if a girl thinks she's hot stuff, guys will treat her like she's hot stuff."

I made a face. "You mean stuck-up? That doesn't make much sense."

Tina shrugged. "I don't know. Alexa says if you don't believe in yourself, nobody else will believe in you. Oh my gosh, look, they're hugging again!" Tina reported, grabbing my arm. "This is so romantic! Maybe they've been in love for years, but their parents have kept them apart, kind of like Romeo and Juliet! Do you think he'll kiss her right here in the lounge?"

At that moment, Dad came striding back into the lounge. The first thing he saw was Veronica, and he went right over to her. Then he pointed across the room to me, and she realized I was in the room for the first time.

"Look who I found," Dad said happily, leading Veronica over to us.

"I was just about to go to Heidi's room to look for you," Veronica said.

"I guess we don't need to introduce you to Brad," Tina said, dimples showing through her smirk.

"Oh, you know my cousin?" Veronica asked with surprise.

"Cousin?" I echoed.

Veronica nodded. "His mother is my mother's sister," she explained. "That has a lot to do with why my mother took the job here in Hope." She waved Brad over to us, and quickly everyone was introduced to everyone else.

"Hi, Dr. Dan," Tina said with a big grin.

"You know my father?" I asked with surprise.

"I hang out in pediatrics a lot," Tina explained. "All the kids love you there," she added to my dad.

"They love you, too," Dad told her.

Terrific. Everyone was loving everyone else, and here was another person my dad knew whom I knew absolutely nothing about. I didn't like it and I didn't know why.

"What do you do over there?" I asked Tina, and I could hear that my voice sounded kind of cold.

"Play with the kids and stuff," Tina said easily. "Sometimes we put on shows for them." She turned to Dad. "Remember that talent show we did where you dressed up like the head nurse? That was just about the funniest thing I ever saw in my life!"

"Virginia didn't think so," Dad said ruefully.

"She doesn't have much of a sense of humor," Brad said with a small smile.

I checked Brad out without letting on that I was checking him out, if you know what I mean. Up close, he was much cuter than he'd seemed from far away, and he had a great shy smile. Maybe he and I would fall madly in love, and then I'd never think about Trevor again. Or maybe Trevor would see us together and just seeing me with an actual guy would suddenly make Trevor appreciate that I really was a girl, and—

". . . so I told her you'd come to her room right away," Dad finished.

"What?" I asked, since I'd missed most of what he'd said.

"I said Heidi's awake and she looks much better," Dad repeated. "She asked for you and I told her you'd be right there."

"Oh, that's great!" I cried. "My little sister," I added, for Brad's benefit.

"Hey, can I come meet your sister?" Tina asked eagerly.

"Sure," I said.

"I'd like to come, too, if it's all right," Veronica said softly.

Tina turned to Brad. "Want to come?" she asked eagerly.

"Nah," Brad said, but he said it like he really did want to come.

"Oh, sure you do," Tina said, linking her arm through his. "We'll all go together!"

Brad smiled, his pale skin flushing a little. "You talked me into it."

And so Dad, Brad, Veronica, Tina, and I headed back to pediatrics, to visit Heidi, who was awake and asking for me.

Now, if only Jennifer was on one side of me and Trevor had his arm around me, everything would be perfect.

"So, Brad, have you lived in Hope a long time?" Tina asked as we headed for the kids' wing.

"Since I was ten," he reported. "I was born in Boston. We used to spend a lot of time in New York, though."

"Our mothers are very close," Veronica explained. "Aunt Gwen is an artist."

"Oh, so that's where you get your talent," Tina told Brad as we rounded the corner.

"What talent?" Brad asked.

"I saw your painting," Tina said. "It was great."

Brad shrugged. "It always seems to turn out different on the paper than it is in my mind, you know?"

"Oh, sure, I understand completely," Tina assured him.

Wow, was she ever comfortable around guys! I was impressed. Why couldn't I be more like that? Why did I have to get all tongue-tied and stupid? And Tina didn't even go to school, so she didn't get to practice on any guys on a regular basis!

"So, you don't seem very sick," Tina said. "But then, I have lupus, and people always tell me that, too."

Brad smiled at her a little. "So you know what it's like."

"Well, I know what it's like for me," Tina said. "I don't know what's wrong with you."

Brad just shrugged and turned to me.

"So, what's wrong with your little sister, anyway?" he asked, quickly changing the subject.

Well, whatever was wrong with Brad it was pretty clear he didn't want to talk about it. Still, even though I hadn't known Tina for very long it was pretty obvious that if anyone could pry it out of him, it would be Tina I'm-Not-Shy Wu.

"I can't decide which of you girls is the foxiest," Jerome said, limping over to us on his crutches. He wriggled his eyebrows at us. "I'll have to take all of you out."

"Hey, Jerome, on Monday you told me I was the cutest girl in here!" Tina exclaimed, pretending to pout.

"They're just visiting," Jerome pointed out. "That means you don't have as much comp."

She threw the paper from her straw at him.

It was an hour later, and Veronica, Tina, and I were sitting in the kids' playroom, drinking Cokes we'd gotten from the Coke machine down the hall.

I idly looked around as I stirred my Coke with the straw. Everything in the huge playroom was done in bright colors, to make it more cheerful-looking, I figured. Four kids sat together on a large red couch, watching cartoons on the TV. In the corner was a sandbox with pails and shovels. A playpen area had building blocks and huge neon plastic pipes that snapped together. There was an art table and a reading corner, and a big chair marked "THE WISHING CHAIR." It was a nice room, but it wasn't nearly as fabulous as the Foxes Den.

I was actually starting to feel better about everything. Heidi really *did* look much better. Brad was quiet but nice, and he'd paid attention to me before he went back to the Foxx Wing. I liked Tina better than any girl I'd met in a long time. She was so enthusiastic and funny! I still wasn't so crazy about Veronica, but her mom *did* save Heidi's life, and that had been all Veronica's idea.

"What's the Wishing Chair?" I asked Tina.

"It's a kind of therapy," Tina explained. "A kid sits in the chair and says whatever their most secret wish is."

"To get better, I would think," Veronica said.

"You'd be surprised," Tina said. "A lot of times they say things like they wish their parents wouldn't be so worried about them, or they wish their daddy had enough money. It's really amazing." She cocked her head at me. "The chair was your dad's idea."

"No kidding?" I marveled.

Tina nodded. "The kids really love him."

"Yeah, he's pretty cool," Jerome agreed. "So, how's my new girlfriend today?"

"I'm not your girlfriend," I said, blushing. I knew it was stupid, letting a ten year old make me blush, but I couldn't help it.

"We're having a secret romance," he told Tina and Veronica.

"Hey, I thought I was your girlfriend!" Tina protested.

"Please, don't fight over me," Jerome said solemnly. He looked Veronica up and down. "You're very fine, pretty momma."

Veronica looked at me. "Who is this?"

"Jerome," I said. "He's ten."

"Ten and a half," Jerome corrected, having a seat next to Veronica. "I have my own gang," he told her. "We're fierce."

"I wouldn't mess with you," Tina agreed.

"Aw, we don't hurt girls," Jerome said. "Hey, remember that time you put on a show for us?"

Tina nodded. "You mean my rap version of Snow White and the Seven Dwarfs," she said with a laugh.

"Yeah, that was bad, man," Jerome said. "I mean, the little kids liked it."

"Oh, come on, you liked it, too," Tina teased him.

"When are you gonna do another show?" Jerome asked eagerly.

Brianna and another little girl toddled over to the table. She climbed into Tina's lap.

"Hi, cutie," Tina said, kissing Brianna on the top of her bald head.

"Can we be in a play with you again, Tina?" the other little girl asked, grabbing Tina's hand.

"The kids got to be the dwarfs in my play," Tina explained. "This is Deena. She played Grumpy."

"I was mad at everyone!" Deena said in a gruff voice.

"Heidi would love that," I said. "Maybe you could put on another show."

"Yeahhhh!" Deena and Brianna yelled happily.

"Maybe you could help me," Tina suggested.

"Not me," I replied. "I have absolutely no acting talent. The only thing I'm good at is gymnastics."

"Like in the Olympics?" Jerome asked, his

face lighting up. "Those gymnastic girls are fierce!"

"Well, I'm not that good," I admitted. "But I'm on the team at school, or at least I was last year."

"Hey, I just got a great idea," Tina said. "What if we put on a variety show!"

"Yeahhhh!" Deena and Brianna yelled again.

"What's a variety show?" Brianna asked.

"Where people do different acts," Tina explained to the little girl. "One person sings and one person dances—"

"And one person does gymnastics!" Jerome said. "Do you wear one of those tight leotards?" He wiggled his eyebrows at me.

"Gross!" I cried.

"I think it's a great idea," Veronica said.

"Good," Tina said. "You can be in it with us."

"Me?" Veronica asked, clearly shocked. "Oh no, not me."

"Why not you?" I asked her. "You're supposed to be this great ballet dancer, aren't you?"

"Well, yes," Veronica agreed. "But I'm practically a professional—"

"Oh, so you couldn't lower yourself to be

in a variety show for kids at Hope Hospital?" I asked her.

"Hey, do you wear one of those short, little skirt things?" Jerome asked, wiggling his eyebrows again.

"You're a ballerina?" Brianna asked Veronica, her eyes huge.

"Yes, I am."

"I wish I could be a ballerina," Brianna said softly.

"You're too sick," Deena told her, curling a lock of her black hair around one finger.

"I know," Brianna said. "But when I get better I can be a ballerina." She gave Veronica a dreamy look. "You're as pretty as a princess."

"Thank you," Veronica said.

"I wish I could see you dance," Brianna added shyly.

"You can," Tina told Brianna. "Because Veronica is going to be in a show right here at the hospital. Aren't you, Veronica?"

"Well, I—"

"You wouldn't want to disappoint Brianna and Deena, would you?" Tina asked.

"Please-please-please-please-please," the two little girls wheedled.

"Okay, okay, I'll do it," Veronica said.

"Yeahhhh!" Brianna and Deena yelled.

"Cool!" Jerome put in.

"If you two do it, too, that is," Veronica added, looking at me.

"Cindy?" Tina asked.

"Does anyone ever say no to you?" I asked Tina.

"Not often," she said with a big grin. "Oh, you guys, this is going to be a total blast! You'll see! And the kids will love it! We'll have to rehearse and—"

"Hold on there," I interrupted. "I've got tons of homework to do, and this play thing for social studies . . ."

"And I've got to get two hours of ballet in every day," Veronica said.

"So, there are twenty-four hours in every day," Tina said cheerfully. "We'll work it out!"

CHAPTER 9

"Jerome, time for your meds!" Rachel Dander sang out, bouncing over to us. She was carrying some pills for Jerome in a little paper cup.

"Oh, man," he groaned. "I don't need that stuff, woman!"

I looked at my watch. It was an hour later. Veronica, Tina, and I had gotten so involved in planning the variety show for the kids that I'd completely lost track of time.

We had decided to put the show on in a week. I figured Heidi would be a lot better by then, and she'd be able to come into the playroom and see the show. Tina was going to be the MC, and she planned to do a rap version of Little Red Riding Hood. I would do a gymnastics routine to a rocking tune by Pearl Jam, and Veronica would dance to "I Will Always Love You."

I was surprised when she picked that, because it was Heidi's favorite song. She loved to sing along with Whitney Houston and pretend she was a famous star. Veronica told me she remembered Heidi saying it was her favorite song, and that was why she'd picked it.

Huh. Maybe it was possible that I underestimated her at times.

Rachel wagged her finger at Jerome. "Come on now, Jerome," she chided him. "Remember, a frown is just a smile turned upside down!"

"Oh, man—" Jerome protested.

"I need to take some blood, too, so we have to go back to your room. I promise to sprinkle the needle with magic fairy dust so it won't hurt!"

Jerome stood up on his one leg and stuck his crutches under his arms. "Man, when I get out of here nobody is gonna come near me with a needle ever again. Stay sweet, ladies." He limped away on his crutches and actually managed to look cocky at the same time. Rachel reached out to help him but he feinted away from her.

"He's the greatest kid," Tina said, watching him leave.

"He's an original, I'll give you that!" I said. "My dad said he lost his leg because of bone cancer."

Tina nodded. "He's very sick—that's what I heard."

"I'd hate being around sick people all the time," I said with a shudder. "It's just so creepy and depressing!"

Oh my God. How could I have said that? Because I had forgotten that Tina was sick, that's how.

"Tina, I'm sorry," I said quickly, "I didn't mean—"

"That's okay," she said easily.

"It's just that you don't even seem sick—"

"Like I said, you caught me on a good day," she admitted.

"What's wrong with you?" Veronica asked.

"Lupus," Tina replied. "It's this autoimmune disease—"

"Where your immune system attacks the various systems of your body as if they were disease," Veronica finished for her. "I know."

"Wow!" Tina exclaimed. "I'm impressed!"

"I read my mom's pediatric medical books for fun sometimes," Veronica admitted.

"That's your idea of *fun?*" I asked her.

"Yes," she said. "I hate reading fiction, but I love to read about medicine. That and ballet are really all I care about."

"Veronica, no offense, but you are very strange," I told her.

"No offense taken," she replied seriously.

"Well, I hate to read," Tina said. "Except for romance novels, that is."

Rachel stuck her head in the door of the playroom. "Excuse me, Cindy, but where's your dad?"

"In with Heidi," I replied. "I'm supposed to meet him here."

"Thanks, sweet pea!" she chirped, and disappeared.

"She just called me 'sweet pea'," I said. "Get me the hurl bag."

"Of course you know she's madly and passionately in love with your father," Tina told me, slurping up some Coke through her straw.

"Get out of here!" I replied with disgust.

"It's true!" Tina insisted. "He even went over to her apartment for dinner last week."

"He did not," I said irritably. "Don't you think I'd know if my own father went over to her apartment for dinner?"

"The kids are always the last to know," Tina said with conviction.

"I would hate it if my mother started dating," Veronica said with a shudder.

"Your parents split up?" Tina asked.

Veronica nodded and sighed. "It just happened. The papers aren't even final yet."

"You think they'll get back together?" Tina asked.

"I wish," Veronica said. She pushed her hair behind one ear. "The whole thing is my mother's fault. She's so devoted to medicine that she never had time for my father or for me."

"But I thought you told me your dad is a doctor, too," I said.

Veronica nodded. "But at least he came home at night. Mom was always at the hospital. I never saw her at all. She cares about her patients a lot more than she ever cared about me or my father. She barely even knows what grade I'm in."

"That sounds like heaven to me," Tina said, chewing on her straw. "I have this big Chinese family—"

"Did you grow up in China?" I asked.

Tina gave me a look. "Do I sound like I grew up in China?" she asked.

I blushed. She sounded just as American as I do. "Dumb question," I mumbled.

"Oh, it's okay," Tina said with a laugh. "I get asked stuff like that all the time. My grandparents are from Singapore, actually, but I was born in San Francisco. We moved to Hope two years ago when my dad got his doctorate."

"Does he work here at the hospital?" Veronica asked.

Tina nodded. "He's here all the time and my mom is home all the time, which is excruciating. My grandparents from Singapore live with us, too. Everyone knows what everyone else is doing every minute of the day. I can't even breathe in private!"

"It sounds wonderful," Veronica said wistfully.

"Well, it isn't," Tina assured her. "And on top of that, my dad is a child psychologist, so he analyzes me all the time!"

"Now that I would hate," I told her.

"It's terrible!" Tina agreed. "I'd love to have Dr. Dan for a father! You must have fun all the time!"

I just shrugged, since I didn't want to say anything bad about Dad. It was one thing to have fun, I wanted to say, and another thing to never get to be serious. I thought about the Wishing Chair. Why was it Dad could be serious at work but not at home with us?

"Your father is extremely cute," Tina added.

"Please," I snorted, "he's my father!"

"You can't imagine how many of the nurses here are crazed for him," Tina said knowingly.

"Look, no offense, Tina, but you don't know what you're talking about," I told her.

"In matters of the heart, I am an expert," Tina replied.

"My dad doesn't even date!" I exclaimed.

"Is he home every night?" Tina asked.

"Well, no," I admitted.

"Do you know where he is every time he's not home at night?"

"Not exactly," I said. "I mean, he always leaves a phone number—"

"But he doesn't say who is at that phone number with him!" Tina said triumphantly. "Such as Rachel!"

I did not like the way this conversation

was going at all. "Look, if my dad was dating I would know it, okay?"

Tina reached over and touched my hand. "I didn't mean to make you mad or anything," she said. "Sometimes I should just keep my mouth shut."

"Forget it," I said tersely. "Let's just change the subject."

"Okay," Tina said easily. "Let's talk about Brad!"

And even though Brad was a subject I was very interested in, I didn't pay much attention. I was too busy thinking about what Tina had said about my father. Was it actually possible that my dad was dating and keeping it a secret from me?

I was finding out there was a lot about my dad and his life that I didn't know at all.

And I didn't like that one bit.

CHAPTER 10

"Hi, Cindy. Hi, Veronica!" Heidi said brightly. "Rachel made me a puppet!"

"Hi," Rachel said from the foot of Heidi's bed. She was holding a girl puppet with bandages on her head, just like Heidi's.

It was two days later, and Miss Jenkins had given me and Veronica a ride over to the hospital after school. We planned to work on our play for social studies, and then get together with Tina to do some more work on our variety show. Even though I was spending time with Veronica, I can't say I really liked her. She was just so perfect-looking, and she was so serious all the time.

We never talked about the whole thing with Trevor. At school I saw them together, like at lunch time, for instance, but I ignored them.

Trevor would try to talk to me, but I still refused. I knew it was stupid and way immature, but I couldn't help myself. I missed being friends with him, but I was too mad and embarrassed to do anything about it.

I noticed that Veronica was looking gorgeous as always. She managed to look as if she made no effort to look perfect but she looked perfect anyway. I hate girls like that. She had on a long red and black flannel shirt, black stretch leggings and little black ballet flats. Her gorgeous hair was held back by a slender red ribbon. I looked down at my own outfit—jeans and a University of Michigan sweatshirt, with high top sneakers on my feet. I had put my hair in a ponytail that morning, but as usual the curls had escaped and fell around my face. And I had ink stains all over my right hand from when my pen had leaked in algebra. Who could blame Trevor for loving Veronica The Perfect instead of Cindy The Ink-Stained Shrimp?

Life was simply not fair.

I vowed not to think about Veronica, to

concentrate on my little sister. After all, Veronica didn't even have a little sister.

"Can I keep the puppet, Rachel?" Heidi asked hopefully.

"Of course," Rachel said. She took the puppet off her hand and gave it to Heidi. "She's yours now."

At that moment a little bald face appeared in the doorway. It was Brianna. "Can I come in?" she asked shyly.

"Of course," Rachel told her brightly. "The more the merrier!"

Brianna toddled over to Heidi's bed, expertly dragging her IV with her. It seemed to me her walk was more unsteady, and she looked even puffier than she had looked before. "Hi," she said to Heidi. "I'm Brianna."

"I'm Heidi," my sister said, looking at the other little girl curiously. "You're bald, too."

Brianna nodded. "I used to have blond hair."

"Me, too," Heidi said. "Did you fall off a Ferris wheel, too?"

Brianna shook her head no. "I have cancer," she explained.

Heidi looked horrified, and I knew what she had to be thinking. Mom. Dying of cancer.

"There's lots of different kinds of cancer,"
I told Heidi quickly. "Lots of people who
have cancer get well."

"I'm gonna get well," Brianna said.

"How do you know?" Heidi asked in a
guarded voice.

Brianna thought about it a minute. "Dr.
Dan told me so," she finally said. "He
wouldn't lie to me." She popped her head
under Heidi's bed and looked around, then
she popped back up again. I had no idea
what she was doing.

"He can't make you better," Heidi said
solemnly. "He couldn't make my mom
better, and that was his wife."

Brianna drew a pattern on Heidi's
bedspread with her finger. "I know he can't
make me better," she mumbled. Then she
looked up. "But I'm just a little girl, and
your mom was a grown-up."

I gulped hard and looked away from
them. Little kids could die, too. Anyone
could die at any time. Anyone.

"When you get better we could play,"
Brianna offered.

"Okay," Heidi said. She put the puppet
Rachel had given her on her hand and
made it look at her. "You were a bad girl,"
she told the puppet.

"Why do you think that?" Rachel asked.

"Because she got hurt," Heidi said. "She got hurt because she was bad."

I sat down on Heidi's bed. Brianna looked at me, her eyes huge. She stuck one finger in her mouth.

"Do you think you were bad?" I asked Heidi carefully.

Heidi shrugged and looked at me from under her lashes. "You told me not to jump around," she said softly.

I carefully wrapped my arms around her. "Oh, honey, you weren't bad! Something was wrong with the safety bar! You didn't do anything wrong!"

"But you said—"

"No!" I cried. "You're a good girl and you didn't do anything wrong!"

Rachel gave me a dazzling smile. "What a wonderful big sister you are!"

"I'm just telling her the truth," I replied stiffly. I didn't like Rachel and I didn't see any reason I should be nice to her. I mean, according to Tina she was secretly going out with my father. What kind of woman does a thing like that? And on top of that, she acted really goofy, like she'd just stepped out of some kids' fairy tale. She was just so sweet she made my teeth hurt.

"Hey, you guys!" Tina said, popping her head in the door. She had on an oversized red sweater and baggy red and white checked pants, and she looked really darling. "Hi, Brianna! How are you doing, Heidi?"

"I had ice cream," Heidi said happily.

"Yum!" Tina exclaimed.

"Are you gonna practice your show today?" Heidi asked Tina eagerly.

"Sure we are," Tina said. "We're going to have a special part for you in it, too."

We had told Heidi about the variety show we were going to put on, and she was very psyched about it.

"But I can't," Heidi said. "I can't even move my legs."

"You can wear the princess crown we're going to make for you, though," Tina said. "You'll be the princess of the entire show."

"Could I be a princess, too?" Brianna asked hopefully.

"But of course," Tina replied. "Two princesses, very good casting on your part."

"I want to be the only princess," Heidi said stubbornly.

"Now, now, Heidi," Rachel chirped, "sharing is caring!"

I looked at Brianna thoughtfully. "Maybe Heidi could be the princess this time, and you could be the princess the next time."

"That would be okay, I guess," Brianna said. She turned to Tina. "Can I be the princess next time, all by myself?"

"Absolutely," Tina promised.

"Will next time be soon?" Brianna asked.

"Oh, sure," Tina assured her. "We'll put on lots of shows!"

I shot Tina a look. I had no intention of putting on "lots of shows," and I was pretty sure Veronica didn't either.

"I have to go now," Brianna said. She turned to Heidi. "Can I come back and see you later?"

"Okay," Heidi agreed.

Brianna cocked her head to one side. "We're friends now, right?"

"Right," Heidi replied.

Brianna gave Heidi a smile that lit up the room. "We'll both be pretty again soon. You'll see." She turned to Rachel. "Could you make sure the light is on in my room tonight when it gets dark?"

"Of course," Rachel agreed.

Brianna twisted her foot anxiously. "Sometimes when it gets dark, I get scared. And I think a big monster is under the bed."

"I'll come check for monsters," Rachel promised.

"Okay," Brianna agreed. "Bye, Heidi! Oh, I checked under your bed for you. No monsters." Then she turned and toddled out the door.

"That's an amazing child," Veronica said.

"She's my new friend," Heidi explained happily. Then she got a pensive look on her face. "I don't think either one of us should be the princess, really."

"No frowns!" Rachel said gaily.

"I can't be a princess," Heidi explained, "because a princess has long, beautiful hair, like Veronica."

"Your hair will grow back," I told Heidi. "So will Brianna's."

"I hate this ugly bandage," Heidi said sadly.

"Well, let's face it, white is not exactly your color," Tina said. She folded her arms and walked around the bed, looking at Heidi. "I say we do something about it. I'm seeing . . . pink. Yes, definitely something in pink."

"Pink is my favorite color!" Heidi yelled.

"Because you have wonderful taste," Tina agreed. "Now, I, myself, look like dogmeat in pink. But pink is perfection for you. I'll be right back." She took off out of the room like a flash.

"Where did she go?" Heidi asked, wide-eyed.

"I don't know," I said.

Rachel stood up and straightened Heidi's covers. "I'm just going to go check on some of the other boys and girls, but I'll be back soon, okay?"

"Okay," Heidi agreed. She yawned. "Brianna will come back and see me later, won't she?"

"I'm sure of it," Veronica told her.

"I like her," Heidi said, yawning again. "I'm glad she checked for monsters. I'm getting sleepy."

"That's good," Rachel told her. "You rest." She turned to me. "You have a very wonderful family."

"They're okay," I said.

"Your father is a wonderful man," she continued in that earnest voice.

"Well, he's not really a doctor or anything," I pointed out.

"Oh, but he's so . . . so wonderful!" she gushed. "So caring and compassionate, and funny and dear!"

"Yeah, whatever," I said, since I had no idea in the world what I was supposed to say.

"I just wanted you to know how much I . . . I mean how much *we* here at the hospital care for him," Rachel said, her eyes shining. "Well, I'll see you girls later."

I made a face. "Major yuck factor!"

Veronica sniffed the air after Rachel left. "She's wearing too much perfume, don't you think?"

"I don't want to think about her at all," I said. I turned to Heidi. "Want us to let you sleep and come back later?"

"No," Heidi said. "Don't go." She moved around a little, which was about as much as she could move. "My legs hurt."

"I know, honey," I said.

"I want to go home." Her lower lip began to quiver, and soon tears were cascading down her cheeks.

I put my arms around her, careful not to hurt her. "You'll go home when you're better, Heidi. Don't cry!"

"B-B-But I want to go home now!" Heidi cried. "I want to sleep in my own bed!"

I felt so helpless and so guilty. "Shh, it's okay, Heidi," I said. "We all love you. And Clark is coming over later to see you. You'll like that."

"I want to go home!" she wailed, truly sobbing now. "I want Daddy!"

"Want me to do find him?" Veronica offered.

"Would you?"

"Sure," she said. "I'll be right back."

"Hold it! Hold everything!" Tina cried, running into the room before Veronica could get out the door. She ran over to Heidi. "I'll be very careful," she said, as she wrapped the long piece of pink fabric she was holding around Heidi's head. "You strike me as a girl who likes hearts, am I right?" Tina asked Heidi.

"I like hearts," Heidi said in a little voice. She was still shuddering, but she had stopped crying.

"Ta-da!" Tina cried, pulling two plastic hearts out of her pocket. We simply pin these to your gorgeous head-wrap like so . . ." She carefully pinned the hearts onto the pink fabric, then she stood back to survey her work.

"Can I see?" Heidi asked eagerly.

Veronica found a hand mirror on the dresser and gave it to Heidi.

"You look fabulous!" Tina told her. "You are the best looking thing in this entire hospital! *Très fashionable!*"

"What does 'tray' mean?" Heidi asked.

"It's 'very' in French," Tina explained. "Every boy in here will fall madly in love with you now. Don't be surprised if people think you are a famous movie star and ask for your autograph!"

Heidi giggled and looked at herself in the mirror some more. "Can I still be the princess in your show?"

"Absolutely," Tina said. "We'll be sure to make your crown pink, Your Highness."

"I'm kind of tired now," she said, and her eyes began to droop shut.

"Let's let her sleep," I whispered. I kissed Heidi on the forehead. "We'll be back," I told her.

"Cinderella?" she whispered.

"What, honey?"

"I love you," Heidi said. By the time we snuck out of the room her eyes were already closed.

"Excuse me, but did your little sister just call you *Cinderella*?"

"Yeah," I said with a sigh.

"But your name isn't really—" Veronica began.

"Yes, it is, really," I said. "And if either one of you tells anyone, your life won't be worth living."

"Your secret is safe with me," Veronica said solemnly.

"But it's the coolest name!" Tina said, cracking up. "Do you have a brother named Prince Charming?"

"I have a brother named Clark, as in Clark Kent, actually," I admitted.

"I guess both of your parents had a sense of humor," Veronica said.

"If you could call it that." I turned to Tina. "Listen, what you did in there with Heidi was great. You're wonderful with kids. Where did you get that stuff?"

"There's a big box of material and all kinds of junk at the Foxes Den," she explained as we walked down the hall. "Some fabric store donated it. I think it's supposed to be for art therapy or something, but no one ever uses the stuff."

"Hi, girls!" Dad said, bounding over to us. "I was just going in to check on Heidi."

"She's asleep," I told Dad, and gave him a kiss on the cheek.

"Well, that's good," he said. "So what are you three up to?"

"Veronica and I have to work on our play for social studies," I explained. "Then we're rehearsing for the variety show on Saturday."

We had already told Dad about the show we were planning, because we had to get permission from the pediatric unit.

"Hey, you guys want me to juggle?" Dad asked eagerly.

"That would be great!" Tina cried.

"I could dress up as a clown," Dad said. "The kids love it when I do that. And Rachel could wear her Tinker Bell costume!"

I practically choked. "Rachel has a Tinker Bell costume?"

"The littlest kids just love it when she wears it," Dad said. "It's really cute."

"I'll bet," I said deadpan, but my sarcasm was completely lost on my father.

"It'll be a blast!" Dad said. "I'm just going to look in on Heidi, then I'll be in the kids' playroom if you need me. Oh, by the way, Cin, I'll be a little late tonight. I've got a meeting. Do you mind?"

Tina gave me significant look, which I chose to ignore.

"What kind of meeting?" I asked sharply.

"Just a hospital thing," he said.

"Ask if Rachel is going to be there," Tina hissed in my ear.

"Shut up!" I hissed back.

"Oh, Mr. Winters!" Dr. Langley called, striding down the hallway toward us. "I'd like to talk to you about Heidi."

"That has to be your mom," Tina said to Veronica. "She looks just like you!"

"Hello, Veronica," Dr. Langley said. "What are you doing here?"

"School work with Cindy," Veronica said. She introduced her mother to Tina.

"Nice to meet you," Dr. Langley said in that formal way that she and Veronica both had. She turned to my father. "Shall we go down the hall and talk?"

"Your mother is a babe," Tina told Veronica, as she watched Dr. Langley and my dad head down the hall together.

"She's attractive, I suppose," Veronica said. "It doesn't seem very important."

"Ha, that shows what you know," Tina said. Then her eyes lit up. "Oh my gosh, I just got the most brilliant idea!"

Veronica and I looked at her expectantly.

"About your father!" Tina said excitedly. "I just got the most brilliant plan to get him away from the clutches of Rachel Dander!"

"What?" I asked.

"Simple!" Tina exclaimed. "We make sure he falls in love with Veronica's mother! Now, am I a genius, or what?"

CHAPTER 11

"That is a terrible idea!" Veronica yelled.

"Really terrible!" I agreed vehemently.

"Fine, leave him in the clutches of Tinker Bell," Tina said airily.

"He's not in anyone's clutches!" I insisted. "He doesn't even date!"

"Neither does my mother," Veronica said firmly.

"Okay, forget I said anything," Tina said. "Let's go back to the Foxes Den and see if Brad's there."

We walked down the hall toward the Foxx Wing, following the red arrow on the floor.

"My mother and Cindy's father don't even have anything in common," Veronica said huffily.

"That's right," I agreed. "My dad is a joke-a-minute kind of guy, and Veronica's mom is totally serious all the time."

"Opposites attract, you know," Tina said as we rounded the corner.

"It's a truly dumb idea, Tina," I said.

"Okay," Tina said. "But if you end up with Glenda the Good Witch as your stepmother, don't say I didn't warn you!"

Veronica shuddered. "Can you imagine?"

"My dad is not marrying anyone," I insisted. "He's not even dating anyone!"

"And he's certainly not dating my mother!" Veronica added.

I could have obsessed about this whole thing with my dad for a lot longer, if right at that moment I hadn't seen Trevor Wayne walking toward us. He had a blue stuffed bunny in his hands.

"Wow, seriously cute," Tina whispered as Trevor walked toward us. "And I'm not talking about the bunny."

"Hi," he said giving me a guarded look.

"Hi," I said.

"Hello," Veronica said in her soft voice.

"I was on my way to Heidi's room. My

brother parked in the back parking lot and I got kind of lost."

"She's asleep," I said in a cold voice.

"Oh." He twisted the bunny's ear around in his fingers. "I could wait, I guess . . ."

"Hi, there!" Tina said. "I'm Tina Wu. Who are you?"

"Trevor Wayne," he said.

"Oh, you're the guy Veronica is dating!" Tina cried.

"We're just friends," Veronica said quickly.

"I'm so sure," I muttered under my breath.

"It's true!" Veronica insisted. "I told you I wouldn't go out on a date with him! Did you think I was lying to you?"

"So what were you doing at the fair together?" I demanded. "I saw you, you know!"

"That wasn't a date!" Veronica insisted.

"Hey, Winters, is that what you've been all bugged about?" Trevor demanded.

My face burned with embarrassment. "I don't care what either one of you do! Why would I care?"

"Look, Veronica is telling you the truth," Trevor insisted. "We aren't a couple or anything—"

"Hel-lo, Earth to Trevor!" I yelled. "I don't care!"

"I think you do," Veronica said.

"I should have kept my mouth shut, I can see that," Tina said, biting her lower lip. "Can everyone just pretend I never said a word?"

"I get it now!" Trevor said. "You've been ticked off at me because you think I'm dating Veronica!"

"I don't care who you date, Trevor Wayne!" I yelled.

"There's nothing for you to feel jealous about," Veronica said earnestly. "I know you like Trevor—"

"I hate Trevor!" I cried.

"But Cin and me are just buds," Trevor insisted. "That's why none of this makes any sense—"

"Can't you see she likes you as more than a friend?" Veronica asked him. "I tried to tell you—"

"Just leave me alone!" I yelled. And then before I even knew I was going to do it, I was running down that hall, as far away from their staring, gaping faces as I could possibly get.

My plan was to never come out of the bathroom.

I locked myself in a stall in the first ladies room I came to. Unfortunately my plans to live out my life in stall number three were thwarted when Tina and Veronica came after me.

"Cindy?" Veronica called.

"Cindy?" Tina echoed. "Are you in here?"

I didn't answer.

The next thing I knew Tina's round face was peeking at me from under the door. "Hi," she said.

"Go away!" I hissed. "Can't I even have privacy in the john?"

"But you're not using it, you're hiding," Tina pointed out, her upside-down face still looking up at me.

"Just leave me alone," I insisted, pulling my feet up and hugging my knees.

The next thing I knew Veronica's face was next to Tina's. "Cindy?" she said. "Please come out so I can explain what happened—"

"There's nothing to explain," I said. "Go away."

"But we just want to—" Veronica began.

Just then I heard the door to the ladies room open, and loud voices boomed through the room.

". . . Well, the doctor said it was my sugar,

but I said 'Doctor, no one in my family has a sugar problem' and he said—"

At that moment I heard a deep intake of breath, which I figured meant whoever was talking had just taken in the sight of Veronica and Tina on their knees, peeking under a toilet stall.

"What in heaven's name are you girls doing?" a different woman's voice demanded.

"Uh, looking for my contact lens," Tina improvised. "Do you see it, Veronica?"

"I'm still looking," Veronica assured her.

"It's got to be here somewhere," Tina said.

I ducked my head down, and there were Veronica and Tina crawling around, pretending to look for a contact lens.

"Those things cost a fortune. I hope you find it, dear," the woman said, then she disappeared in one stall and the other woman disappeared into another.

"Let's get out of here!" Tina hissed.

"Come on, Cindy," Veronica said, gracefully getting up from the floor. "Let's go somewhere where we can talk privately."

"All right," I finally agreed. "Move, Tina." She was still on her knees in front of my stall.

"I can't," she said.

"Quit fooling around," I said. "I'll go talk to you guys."

"No, I really can't," she said. "I shouldn't have gotten down here in the first place. Sometimes my joints are too weak for me to . . . uh . . . get up again."

I wanted to help her, but I was stuck inside the stall.

"I'll help you up," Veronica said.

"I'm not such a lightweight, you know," Tina said, trying to sound cheerful. "Pudge is my middle name."

"I'm a dancer and I'm very strong," Veronica said. As I peeked under the stall Veronica got behind Tina and put her hands under Tina's arms. Then she hoisted Tina to her feet.

"Wow, you are strong," Tina said. "Thanks."

I quickly got out of the stall. "Are you okay?" I asked Tina.

"Sure," she said. "Let's go."

We all started walking but Tina was limping.

"You're not okay at all," I told her.

"It's just my knees are kind of weak sometimes," she said, grimacing as she walked.

"Would you like us to get you a wheel-chair?" Veronica offered.

"No, no, I'm fine," Tina insisted. "We can go down to my room and talk." She was limping and we were walking very slowly.

"Where did Trevor go?" I asked casually.

"To Heidi's room," Tina said. "Listen, I'm really sorry I opened my mouth."

"Are you sure you don't want a wheelchair?" Veronica asked Tina again, since it looked as if every step Tina took was painful for her.

"No wheelchair," Tina said vehemently.

"About Trevor—" Veronica began, looking at me.

"You don't have to say anything," I insisted.

"Yes, I do," Veronica said. "I know you like him, and—"

"I don't!"

"Of course you do," Veronica said. "You told me you were almost a couple, remember?"

"Oh, that," I said, blushing furiously. "Well, I might have exaggerated just a little."

"Oh, I already figured that out," Veronica said. "Trevor thinks the two of you are just friends, but you want him to be your boyfriend. Is that about right?"

"No offense, Veronica, but you have the sensitivity of a gerbil."

"No offense taken," Veronica said. "I'm just trying to get the facts straight." She looked at me. "Don't you know I would never, ever go out with the guy you like?"

"Why not?" I asked bitterly. "He doesn't even know I'm a girl."

"Because we're friends, that's why," Veronica said. "I would never, ever do something like that to you."

"But the fair—"

"I wasn't with him," Veronica said.

"Don't lie about it!" I exclaimed. "I saw the two of you—"

"I went alone," Veronica said in a low voice. "Miss Jenkins drove me."

"You went to the fair *alone*?" I repeated.

Veronica nodded, her face flushing with embarrassment. "I would have liked to go with you, but I was afraid to ask you. Then I ran into Trevor at the fair, and I guess that's when you saw us."

I was floored. Totally floored. I didn't know what to say.

"We talked about you a lot," Veronica continued. "Trevor thinks the world of you, you know. I told him I thought you were wonderful, too."

"You did?" I asked, practically too shocked to speak.

Veronica nodded. "And I really do think he'd think of you like a girlfriend instead of just a friend, if you'd give him half a chance."

"That is so romantic!" Tina exclaimed. She took a step, winced and stumbled. Veronica caught her on one side and I caught her on the other. "You guys, I think I really messed up my knee."

"Should I call a doctor or something?" I asked quickly.

But before she could answer me, a voice came over the intercom system.

"Code Blue, Code Blue, Dr. Langley, room 407 Pediatrics, stat."

All the color drained from my face, and the three of us just stared at each other, too shaken to move.

Code Blue meant that someone was in serious trouble, probably dying.

And 407 was Brianna's room.

CHAPTER 12

By the time we got to the pediatric unit doctors and nurses were running into Brianna's room. We could hear loud voices and see the frantic activity. Some of the little kids who were patients stood with us in shock, their faces pale. Some visiting relatives of another little girl looked sad and relieved at the same time. At least it wasn't their kid.

Tina, Veronica, and I stood in the hallway, our bodies pressed against the wall, holding each other's hands as tightly as we could. I prayed as hard as I could, just like when mom died. I knew it was stupid—I mean, it didn't work when my own mother died, so I don't know what made me think it could possibly work for Brianna. But I couldn't help myself.

Jerome stood next to me, balancing himself on his crutches, tears were running down his cheeks. "She can't die, man," he said in his fierce little voice. "God wouldn't be that mean."

Tina put her arm around him.

My father came running down the hall. "It's Brianna?" he asked me.

I nodded.

He cursed under his breath—my father never curses—and he pushed some hair off his face. "I think she'll pull through," he finally said. "Is Rachel in there?"

"I saw her run in just as we got here," Veronica volunteered.

Dad nodded. "She's good. Really good."

I didn't bother to look at him. What difference did it make if Rachel was the most wonderful nurse in the world?

"I didn't mean it when I said she was gonna die," Jerome said, gulping back his tears. "I didn't mean it!"

I bit my lip to keep from crying, myself. "We should have let her be the princess, too," I whispered.

It seemed like forever that we stood there, waiting. Finally Dr. Langley came out of Brianna's room. She walked over to us. "Are Brianna's parents here yet?"

"I haven't seen them," my father said. "But they live on the other side of town. Is she—?"

"I'm sorry," Dr. Langley said. "Brianna didn't make it. She went into complete heart failure. It was very sudden—there was nothing we could do."

"Poor little girl," Dad said, all the color draining out of his face.

"But she can't be dead," Jerome yelled.

"I'm sorry," Dr. Langley said. But she didn't really sound sorry, not to me, anyway. She sounded like it was just another day at the hospital—win a few, lose a few, oh well.

"You killed her!" Jerome yelled at the top of his lungs. "It's your fault, and you don't even care! I hate you!"

"Jerome, Brianna was a very sick little girl," Dr. Langley said quietly. Now I could hear her voice was shaking.

"She did everything she could," Veronica said, touching Jerome's arm.

He shook her off. "I want to see her!"

"I'm sorry, Jerome, you can't," Dr. Langley said firmly.

Jerome looked up at her, his huge brown eyes awash with tears. "You gonna let me die like that?"

Before anyone could answer, he hobbled away on his crutches and went into his room, slamming his door behind him.

All of a sudden I felt like throwing up. Sweat burst out on my forehead and I couldn't breath.

"Cin?" Dad asked. "Are you okay?"

"We should have let her be the princess," I blurted out.

"What, honey?" Dad asked gently.

"Brianna. She wanted to be the princess in the variety show," I said. "But I wanted it to be Heidi. And now . . . now she'll never get to be the princess . . ."

"It's okay, sweetie," Dad said, reaching for me.

"No, it's not okay!" I screamed, shaking him off. "It's not okay when people just . . . just die! What's the point of even living when you have to hurt so much?" I was breathing hard now, panting. I felt as if I wanted to jump out of my skin. If I could have wished myself off the planet Earth I would have.

All the medical personnel in Brianna's room filed out silently. There was only one person still in there. A little girl. All alone.

"It's okay to cry, Cin," Tina said softly, reaching for me.

I stared at Tina. It felt as if something was squeezing my lungs closed, like I couldn't breath. "What do I tell Heidi?" I whispered, as the tears fell down over my cheeks.

"She'll understand—" Dad began.

I turned on him. "No, she won't!" I yelled viciously. "You told her that little girls don't die! Only we both know they *do* die sometimes. You lied to her—"

"I . . . I just didn't want her to worry . . ." Dad faltered. "I wanted to protect her—"

"Well, you didn't protect her very well, did you?" I yelled. "You can't protect anybody! Ever! Ever!"

I started to pound on Dad's chest, the blood roaring in my head. Somehow I knew it wasn't only Brianna I was yelling about, it was Mom. Or maybe it was everything. Everything that was awful and scary that no dad could ever protect you from.

Dad just stood there looking so sad, his hands at his side, letting me hit him.

And then finally, he put his arms around me.

And then I fell over and fainted.

* * *

A funeral for a six year old is the most terrible thing in the world.

The hospital chapel was filled with flowers. Lots of the flowers were pink. I guess that was Brianna's favorite color as well as Heidi's.

It hadn't been easy to tell Heidi about Brianna's death. Dad didn't want to do it. Rachel said she would, but I thought I should be the one. And so I did. Heidi cried. I told her that Brianna was in heaven with Mom, and that made her feel better. It didn't make me feel any better. I don't know if I even believe there is a heaven. I guess I don't understand how the world works at all.

There were lots of people at the funeral. I sat with Dad, Rachel, Veronica, Tina, Trevor, and Brad. Dr. Langley was sitting in the back, along with other people on the hospital staff. I noticed that Jerome was there, dressed up in a black suit. He limped in and sat in the back with a handsome couple who I figured were his parents.

The minister went on and on about how sad it was when someone died so young, but now she was with the angels, blah-blah-blah. How did he know? Maybe Brianna was just plain dead, in the ground, period.

Maybe there was no heaven, and guys like him just pretended there was so we wouldn't all feel scared and bummed out all the time.

Not that I felt scared or bummed out. Not me. I didn't feel much of anything at all. Because I knew the truth. It wasn't safe to love anyone, ever. People died. Good people. Mom. And little Brianna. So what was the point of love? What was the point of anything?

When the minister finished, Brianna's older brother, Greg, made his way up to the front of the church. He unfolded a piece of paper and cleared his throat.

"My little sister, Brianna, was really a great kid," he said in a choked voice. "She was very independent and had a mind of her own. Her favorite color was pink. She would have been happy if everything in the world had been painted pink. She insisted her room be painted pink, and she tried to use the leftover paint to paint our cat, Meow, pink."

People chuckled at that and wiped the tears from their cheeks. Not me. I just sat there.

"She loved beauty pageants and cheerleading and Barbies," Greg continued.

"I guess Brianna was the only person on earth who could get me to play dolls with her." He gulped hard, and the paper in his hands shook.

"Goodbye, Brianna," Greg finished, choking on the words. "You'll live forever in my heart."

People were sobbing loudly as Greg went back to sit with his parents. Tina and Veronica were sobbing, too. Not me.

The minister said a final prayer and the service was over. We went outside—the sun was shining and there wasn't a cloud in the sky. I watched Brianna's family get into a big, black hearse. It struck me that it was kind of a cool car. Brianna would probably have liked to ride in it.

Actually, Brianna *was* riding in it. In the back. Dead.

That thought struck me as being so funny that I started to laugh out loud.

"Honey?" Dad asked, putting his arm around me.

"Oh, nothing," I said. How could I explain? I didn't even know why I had laughed.

"Sometimes laughter is the best medicine," Rachel said, dabbing at her own eyes.

"Shut up," I told her cheerfully.

Dad didn't say a word.

We got into our car, one of a long line of cars that wended their way slowly to the cemetery. We parked and walked to the gravesite, a great, big, empty hole in the ground. Some men carried the casket over to the grave while we all stood around this big hole.

The minister said a few more words, and they lowered the casket into that big hole.

Brianna wouldn't like that. After all, she was just a little girl like my little sister.

And then I remember what she had told us. About the monsters under the bed.

"No, wait!" I screamed. "Brianna's in there!"

"Honey—" Dad said, reaching for me.

I moved away. "She's scared of the dark!" I yelled. "You can't put her in that hole!"

But no one listened to me. The box that held Brianna went lower and lower into the ground, until it landed with a soft thud.

I turned and ran. I didn't know where I was running and I didn't care. I just had to get away. I ran past flowers and trees and lots and lots of graves. I ran until I could hardly fill my lungs with air, then I stopped and fell down on the ground behind a huge tree. I hugged it and I cried so hard I thought my lungs would burst.

I don't know how much time passed before Veronica and Tina found me. They didn't say a word. They just sat down by me, leaning against that big oak tree. For the longest time the three of us just sat there, staring out at nothing, the warm sun shining on our heads.

"My heart— " I finally whispered. I put my hands over the place where it ached, hurt so bad I didn't think I could live.

"I know," Tina said, reaching for my hand.

Veronica reached for my other hand.

"Do you . . ." I gulped hard. "Do you think Brianna's with my mother?"

"I don't know," Veronica said.

"It hurts too much to love people," I gasped, tears cascading down my face.

"What's the alternative?" Tina asked.

"Not caring about anyone, ever," I said fiercely.

"Then what's the point of even being alive?" Veronica wondered.

"I could be more like you," I told her viciously. "You don't care about anyone but yourself." I knew it was mean, but I wanted to be mean. I wanted to hurt someone as much as I was hurting.

"That's not true," Veronica said. "I care about my mother, and about Brad, and about Tina." She gave me a level look. "And I care about you."

"I'm not very nice to you," I admitted.

"I'm not nice all the time, either," Veronica said. She picked a blade of grass. "I guess I can be kind of . . . well . . . serious sometimes. The truth is . . . well, I didn't really have very many friends back in New York."

"Who cares?" I said, sniffing loudly.

"I don't expect you to care," Veronica said. "I'm just telling you the truth. A lot of kids seem to think I'm stuck-up. But I'm not. I'm scared all the time that no one will like me."

"But you're so perfect-looking!" Tina exclaimed.

"Then why am I always so lonely?" Veronica wondered. She looked over at me. "Sometimes I feel really jealous of you for having a brother and a sister."

"I'd gladly give you Clark," I managed.

"No, you wouldn't," Veronica said. "You love him a lot, and I know it. It must be wonderful to have a brother and a sister to love."

I wiped the tears on my cheek with the back of my fist. "Oh sure," I whispered.

"Unless something happens to them. What if something happens to them?"

"You don't have any control over that," Tina said.

"Well, I can't live that way anymore!" I yelled. "I don't want to hurt like this! I want . . . I want my mommy back!"

I cried for a long time, and Tina and Veronica just sat there with me. And then in the distance, I noticed a figure slowly coming toward us. I couldn't make out who it was for a while. And then I realized the person was a kid. A black kid on crutches. With one leg.

"Man, you try doing this with one leg on the grass!" Jerome groused as he hopped over to me. "What you want to make me work so hard for, woman?"

"What are you doing here?" I asked him, trying to shudder out the last of my tears.

"The same thing you're doing here, I guess," Jerome said. He leaned his crutches against the tree and slid to the ground. "Much better."

"Where· are your parents?" Tina asked him.

"I told them to leave," Jerome said. "My gang will come for me, if I call them. They got Harleys."

Harleys, I knew, were a kind of motorcycle. Nobody bothered to challenge that statement, even though we all knew it was ridiculous.

"Pretty nice out here, huh?" Jerome said, staring up at the sun. "Yeah, just me and three fine babes, hanging out in the sun."

"Look, Jerome, no offense," I began, "but this isn't a good time for you to be here."

"I kind of wanted to talk to you," he said, dropping his street voice for a moment. He sounded like a scared, vulnerable little boy.

"What about?" Veronica asked him.

"About your show for the kids at the hospital, what else?" Jerome asked, resuming his "dude" voice.

"That's all over with," I told him.

"How come?" Jerome asked.

"Because I'm never going back there again," I said bluntly.

He picked up a stick and threw it at a nearby tree. "I loved Brianna. She was a really nice little girl." He threw another stick. "There are lots of nice kids at the hospital who are still alive."

"So?" I snapped.

"So . . . I thought maybe you really cared about us—I mean, about them," Jerome said, fighting to sound cool.

"We do," Tina assured him. "But you need to give Cindy some time—"

"I'm never going back there," I said fiercely.

"But, Cindy," Veronica began, "we could—"

"Never," I insisted.

"That's cool," Jerome said, nodding his head. "No biggie. I just wanted to tell you about that new girl, Marielle, though. You know, the one that has sickle-cell anemia?"

I vaguely recalled a little African-American girl, about eight, very skinny and sickly-looking, who had checked into the pediatric wing the day before Brianna died.

"What about her?" Veronica asked.

"She's a really nice girl," Jerome said. "She writes poetry."

"So?" I asked petulantly.

Jerome shrugged. "They think she's gonna die."

"I'm sorry," I said, "but I don't even know her."

"Well, she knows all about you," Jerome said. "Rachel and the other nurses told her. She got real excited about your show and everything."

"We're not doing it."

"Oh, okay," Jerome said. He pushed himself up from the ground with his hands, using the tree for leverage. Then he grabbed his crutches. "I guess you don't care that I'm having surgery next week, either."

"What kind?" Tina asked him with concern.

"Oh, I guess they need to take off my other foot," Jerome said casually. "The cancer got in there. And I thought that, you know, while I was still feeling okay maybe you ladies would be around to see me and put on your show . . ."

No one said anything. Jerome pushed the crutches up under his armpits at a better angle. "Well, it was great to see you foxes again. Stay sweet." Jerome began to limp carefully across the grass.

"Wait!" Tina said. "I'm getting discharged from the hospital on Monday," she told him, "but I'll come back and see you and Marielle."

"I will, too," Veronica said. "We can dance together."

Jerome looked at me. "I really, really like gymnastics," he said. "I bet you look fine in a leotard, momma."

"You're a demented kid!" I said with a laugh.

"I know," he replied with a grin. "I can't help myself."

Everyone stared at me—Veronica, Tina, and Jerome, just waiting.

"Oh, all right," I finally said. "I'll do the stupid show."

Everyone smiled at me. And at that moment I felt the tiniest lifting of the weight on my heart.

CHAPTER 13

I stood to the side of the small stage Dad had fixed up in the hospital playroom and watched Rachel, up there in her Tinker Bell outfit, talk to Dad, who was dressed as a clown. Tina had just finished her Little Red Riding Hood rap, which all the kids loved.

I was dressed in my gymnastics team leotard—blue and white with red stars across the top. Veronica had on a pink leotard and a tutu, and her perfect hair was up in a perfect bun. Tina was dressed like a street Red Riding Hood, in a red sweatshirt with a hood, baggy red sweatpants and red high-top sneakers.

In the crowd was Brad, looking very cute in a blue sweatshirt and jeans, and Trevor, who looked even cuter in a white T-shirt and jean jacket. Trevor smiled at me and I smiled back. He'd written me a letter telling me that he missed being friends with me. Maybe there was hope for us yet. Tina kept grinning at Brad, who grinned back.

I leaned toward her. "You really like him, huh."

"Isn't he terrific?" She sighed, giving him another long-distance smile.

"Did you ever find out what's wrong with him?"

"I asked Veronica," Tina replied. "It has something to do with his heart."

"Is it serious?" I asked, with a familiar feeling of dread lurking in my stomach.

"He's not dying," Tina said quickly.

"But how do you know—"

"Veronica told me," Tina said. "And you know how honest Veronica is."

I nodded. I had to remember that everyone who was sick enough to be in the hospital didn't die. Not Heidi. Not Brad. Not most kids.

"Well, Mr. Clown, if I sprinkle you with magic fairy dust, what will happen to the handkerchief in your pocket?" Rachel was asking Dad.

"Let's find out!" Dad said. Rachel did her fairy dust thing, and Dad pulled on his red handkerchief. It turned into a blue handkerchief, then a green one, then a yellow one. It grew and grew as Dad pulled on it, and the littlest kids laughed and laughed.

"You could blow a lot of noses with that, Mr. Clown!" Rachel trilled.

"This is the hokiest act I ever saw in my life!" I whispered to Tina.

"Tell me about it," she agreed.

"Mr. Clown," Rachel said. "If I give you a kiss, I bet we could find something really, really special in the magic hat!" Rachel kissed my father's white-faced cheek, and then he pulled a real rabbit out of a top hat. The little kids clapped and cheered. And that was strange, because most of them were really, really sick. Half of them were bald from chemotherapy, some of them were in wheelchairs, and yet they looked so happy.

"Isn't Mr. Clown wonderful?" Rachel gushed happily.

"We really do have to get your dad away from Tink," Tina whispered in my ear.

"Just don't fix him up with my mother," Veronica warned.

"You never know what will happen!" Tina sang out happily.

Rachel and Dad finished their act to great applause. Then Tina went to the microphone to introduce me.

"And now boys and girls of all ages," she said, "I present to you gymnast extraordinaire Cindy Winters!"

"Yeahhhh!" the kids yelled, clapping wildly.

The first beats of the rock song filled the air and I took a run toward the stage. Then I did a flip, which went into a cartwheel, and then a leg-over.

"Ooooo," Deena cooed, clapping her hands together. "That was so good!" The new girl, Marielle, shook her head in enthusiastic agreement.

I danced around to the music, doing all the tricks I could think of. The kids loved it, clapping along to the music.

"You looking fine, momma!" Jerome yelled out, and he gave a wolf whistle between his teeth.

I did my final tumble, two slips, and finished in the splits. The whole room burst into applause.

"Wow, you're really good!" Veronica said when I ran back over to her and Tina.

"Thanks," I said, trying to catch my breath.

"You were fantastic!" Tina exclaimed, hugging me hard before she ran back up to the microphone.

"And now for the final act of our show," Tina said, "we have a really special treat. From New York City, please put your hands together for Veronica Langley!"

Everyone applauded, and in the back of the room I noticed Veronica's mom, clapping harder than anyone. Veronica walked over to the microphone and waited for the room to quiet down.

"Thank you," she said. "This dance is dedicated to Brianna Carson, from Heidi Winters."

The first notes to "I Will Always Love You" filled the air.

I looked over at my little sister, who was sitting in the front row in her wheelchair, both legs suspended by an intricate mobile pulley system. She was so brave, and so wonderful, and things had been so tough for her. She was too young to have to struggle with all this life and death stuff. She should be able to just run around, and have fun, and go crying to her mother when things went wrong. Only fate had something different planned, I guess. Something much, much harder. Still, there she was, with a big smile on her little face just the same.

Veronica began to dance. Through my tears I could see all the little kids, mesmerized by the grace and beauty of Veronica, as she danced to Heidi's favorite song.

But as beautiful as Veronica was, I knew that those little kids were even more beautiful. Marielle, who was too weak to get out of her wheelchair, made her arms dance over her head in circles as she watched Veronica. Jerome, who sat near the front, holding Deena on his lap, grinning the biggest grin in the world. And most of all Heidi, my darling Heidi, who still found the courage to smile.

Right then, I realized something. If those kids could go on, I could go on. If they could still have hope, and risk caring and loving, then I could, too.

I couldn't bring Brianna back any more than I could bring Mom back, but there was something I could do. I could keep coming back to the hospital and doing stuff with the kids who were still alive. I had a feeling Brianna would like that. Mom would, too.

When the show was over and the little kids had left the playroom, Veronica, Tina, and I started to clean up.

"That was really good," I told them, as I moved some chairs back around a play table.

"Yeah, the kids loved it," Tina agreed.

"You know, I will have to come back here," I said carefully. "I mean, obviously I'll be here to see Heidi and everything."

"Of course," Veronica agreed.

"We'll want to visit her, too," Tina added.

"And the other kids . . . well, they'd be really disappointed if we, like, never visited them when we're here to see Heidi, don't you think?" I asked.

"You're right," Veronica said. "Deena just asked me if I could read her a story about ballet the night before she has all her new tests done."

"I was thinking . . . maybe we should . . . spend time here, with the kids, you know, stuff like that."

"I'd love that," Tina said, her eyes shining. "We should do it!"

"We should," Veronica agreed. "We really should."

"You won't have as much time for ballet," I warned her.

"So?" she said. "You won't have as much time for gymnastics."

"And I'll have an excuse to get out of the house!" Tina added. "Believe me, between home schooling and lupus, I have zip for a social life!"

"Just the three of us?" I asked them.

"Just us," Veronica agreed.

"It'll be so fantastic!" Tina exclaimed. She hugged Veronica, who looked shocked, and then she hugged me. "I love you guys!"

"Me too," Veronica added shyly.

They both looked at me.

I had a choice. I could be afraid to care, to love ever again, or I could risk it one more time. I didn't really want to do it, it was too hard and too scary. But right at that moment I heard Brianna in my head, and she was laughing. And I remembered something I hadn't been able to remember for the longest time. My mother's smile.

"I love you guys, too," I said, gulping hard.

So it was going to be me, Veronica, and Tina. Girls willing to love, to care, to make a difference, even if we got hurt.

It worked for me.

Dear Reader,

Welcome to my new series, HOPE HOSPITAL. If you've never read any of my books before, thanks for picking up this one! And to my long-time friends, fans, and readers, I hope this new series is everything that you told me you want it to be.

As many of you know, I personally answer each and every piece of mail I get, and I LOVE to hear from all of you out there! I even pick two or three letters to be printed—with your permission only, of course—in the back of each book. If your letter gets picked, I'll send you a free, personally autographed copy of that book.

I really want to know what you think, what you care about, your hopes, joys, and fears, so that I can reflect that in HOPE HOSPITAL. I also line the walls of my office with photos of my readers, so send in those pictures!

Since I often write about best friends, a lot of readers write and ask me if I had best friends who were as terrific as the girls I write about. Yeah! Am I lucky, or what? And one of them, Judy Harris, is still my best friend, even though she lives in New York and I live in Tennessee. Best friends are forever, you guys, so treat yours with love and respect!

So Cherie, babe, you might ask, why ever did you decide to write a new series about girls who do volunteer work at a hospital? Did you ever do volunteer work at a hospital? Nope, I didn't. However, when I was a kid I ran these mysterious fevers for years, and kept getting hospitalized for them. No one ever did figure out what was wrong with me. But I do remember how lonely and scary it was, and how important my best buds were at that time.

We all need to help each other through the scary stuff, right? And we need to help each other celebrate the good stuff. Know what I celebrate? Readers like you. Thank you, thank you, thank you. You are truly the coolest. And I want to hear from you!!!

Cherie

Wanna write to me? The address is:
Cherie Bennett
PO Box 150326
Nashville, Tennessee 37215
Wanna E-mail me? And maybe join in on my monthly contest and gab-fest with moi, my cool husband, Jeff, and my readers from all over the world? Contact me at America Online:
authorchik@aol.com.
Wanna join the Cherie Bennett Believer's Fan Club? Just drop me a note and I'll send you the info!

Cherie Bennett is one of the best-selling authors for young adults and middle readers in the world, with more than three million books in print, in many languages. She is also one of America's finest young playwrights, whose award-winning plays about teens, JOHN LENNON & ME and ANNE FRANK & ME, are being produced around the world. She lives in Nashville, Tennessee, with her husband, Jeff Gottesfeld, a film and theater producer and writer, and their two fat cats, Julius and Trinity.